The Upright Piano Player

DAVID ABBOTT worked for forty years in the advertising industry as a copywriter and creative director. He was a founding partner of Abbott Mead Vickers, the U.K.'s largest advertising agency. He is married, with four children and eight grandchildren. This is his first novel.

The Upright Piano Player

A NOVEL

David Abbott

MACLEHOSE PRESS
QUERCUS · LONDON

First published in Great Britain in 2010 by MacLehose Press
This paperback edition first published in 2011 by

MacLehose Press
an imprint of Quercus
21 Bloomsbury Square
London, WC1A 2NS

A CIP catalogue record for this book is available from the British Library

ISBN 978 1 84916 405 4

2 4 6 8 10 9 7 5 3

Designed and typeset in Caslon by Patty Rennie
Printed and bound in Great Britain by Clays Ltd, St Ives plc

For Eve

The consequences of our actions take hold of us, quite indifferent to our claim that meanwhile we have improved

Nietzsche

the snow doesn't give a soft white
damn Whom it touches

E.E. Cummings

PART ONE

NORFOLK

May 2004

He knew it was unforgivable to drive to the funeral in the old Land Rover, but it was the only transport he had. And anyhow, what difference did it make? What did any of it matter now? The day the police had returned the car he had taken it to the local dealer and they had ripped out the old seat belts and fitted the modern, retractable kind. They had done it in a few hours as an act of kindness, but to him the quick turn-around had felt more like a reproach.

He was not expected at the church. He had told his son that he was not up to it and could not come. That morning, he had found he could not stay away either, and had shaved in a hurry, cutting himself on the neck so that the collar of his white shirt had picked up specks of blood as he fumbled with his tie. A week ago, the doctor had given him sleeping pills, but he did not want oblivion and had not taken them. Now his eyes were almost closed, like those of a boxer at the wrong end of a good left jab, and driving to the church he had strayed on to the verge and mown down fifty yards of cow parsley before regaining the road. Following the arrows chalked on the gateposts, he parked in the meadow next to the church. The sun was high in the sky and the number of red cars in the field depressed him further.

As he walked into the lane he listened for music. There had to be music. It had been a bond between them. Favourite tapes played over and over in the car; a phrase in the lyrics or an exuberant riff prompting delighted laughter, always on cue. He hoped someone had thought about the music – chosen something suitable, not too religious. He would have done it himself – would have done it better than anyone, but they had spared him the task. Get some rest, they had said. Rest?

That night, in the small hours, he had consulted his battered copy of *Hymns Ancient & Modern*. In the index, trying to second-guess his son, he had looked through the list of hymns for special occasions, but he had found evidence only of the Victorians' preoccupation with sin and self-improvement. There were hymns for a temperance meeting; hymns for a teachers' meeting; hymns for the laying of a church foundation stone – but he could find no recommended send-off for a small child dangled from a moving Land Rover.

The church door was closed, but through the open windows he heard the ebb and flow of a prayer and knew that it was too late to go in. He imagined the creak of the door and the click of his heels on the flagged floor, the heads of the congregation scrupulously not turning.

He walked down the path towards the newly dug

grave. The grass matting draped over its sides reminded him of displays in garden centres, overly emphatic in this place of tired turf and ancient stone. The grave's opening seemed almost jocular, little more than a slot in the soil. But then the replays started running in his head and he was sitting on the sofa with his arm around the boy's narrow shoulders and he knew there had been no mistake.

Dear brain, please stop, he pleaded.

He looked around for distraction. The surrounding gravestones bore the name of his daughter-in-law's family. In the next plot, leaning protectively towards the new grave, was the headstone of John and Clara Burnham, the boy's maternal great-grandparents. In a hundred years' time, visitors to this church might wonder how an eight-year-old boy named Cage came to rest here among the long-lived Burnhams.

Then he heard it.

From the church, came the familiar sound of a cha-cha-cha. One night at supper, they had all agreed that Rubén González was the best musician in Cuba. He saw once more the boy slip down from his chair and jig around the kitchen, arms held high, dark hair flying, the back of his head so perfect. He felt ashamed of his worries about the music. Why had he doubted that his son would get it right? God knows, no-one was closer to the boy; no-one loved him more. Not even me, he thought, and I loved him mightily.

The church door opened and he stepped back from the grave. He did not want a place in the front row and retreated to the cover of the blackthorns by the churchyard wall. Two men carried the small coffin on their shoulders while the last chorus of "La Engañadora" spilled out from the church. He realised that his foot was beating time. He stopped it, reassured that no-one could have seen its movement in the long grass. How difficult it must be for the bearers to maintain that slow, measured tread when the music demanded a wilder gait.

Out from the porch came his son and daughter-in-law. She was holding Beth, now two and his only grandchild. Behind them were her parents and her three sisters with husbands, partners and children clustered around them. He knew the Burnhams would overcome this loss, draw together and consolidate. Through the trees he could see the roof tiles of their family home – the house a mere fifty yards from the church, snug in the fold where the lane dips down into the valley. His grandson's grave would be well tended. The Burnham side of the family would not let the boy down.

As the mourners gathered around the grave, his son saw him. There was a small smile of recognition, but no attempt to wave him closer. He stood for a while, not really hearing, not really seeing, and then slipped away through the side gate and back to the car. They had planned a buffet lunch at the Burnhams' after the service, but he would skip that. He could not meet people right now. He sat in the car and closed his eyes. He would rest before driving home.

There was a rap at the window.

"Dad, open the door."

He stirred, almost asleep.

"I've come to get you. You must come."

His son's dear face was the other side of the glass, only inches away. He looked ill, terminally so. Well, he was in a way, wasn't he? Don't they say you never recover from the death of a child? He opened the window and shook his head.

"I can't go in."

"Dad, I need you there."

"Ah, no."

"I need them to know that I haven't lost you as well."

The Burnhams' house was handsome. A white stucco façade, Dutch gables, and the windows and doors arranged with a pleasing symmetry. The sun had shifted, so that the windows of the crowded drawing room were in its full glare. Uncomfortably hot, Henry sat on a low chair that had been brought down from the nursery as emergency seating. He waited patiently for it all to be over. His head was at hip level to the crowd and as long as he did not look up no-one could catch his eye. From time to time, someone patted him on the shoulder and moved on. Two pats were the most common form of sympathetic currency. The vicar had given him just one, but he had left his hand there for a beat longer than anyone else, and there had been the hint of a squeeze. Not knowing what to say, people had said nothing.

He must have nodded off for he was surprised to feel his son's hand cupping his elbow and helping him to his feet.

"Come into the kitchen, Dad, it's quieter there."

He was led to a wing-backed chair by the stove. The cushions yielded to his shape and he closed his eyes. It was three o'clock in the afternoon. He slept for six hours. When he awoke, he saw white plates stacked in columns on the kitchen table and rows of gleaming glasses. The room was tidy and clean. They must have been clearing up around him, talking in whispers, if talking at all. When he stood up he had to hang on to the chair for support. These days, his left knee had a tendency to seize up if not flexed at regular intervals. He aimed a few kicks at an imaginary ball and was able to stand unaided. The kitchen was almost dark, the only light coming from a small lamp on the dresser. They had obviously wanted him to sleep. Their consideration seemed inappropriate.

"Oh, you're ready."

His son came into the room.

"We're taking Beth home now. We can go by yours, if you want."

"No, I've had a sleep. I can get myself home."

His son was suddenly in his arms.

"It was an accident, Dad – an accident."

Henry did not answer, but held him tight. There was the smell of wood smoke in his son's hair and clothes. The family must have lit the fire in the front room, not for the warmth, he thought, but because on a day like this it would be unbearable to contemplate an empty grate. He kissed the soft skin at his son's temple and let him go.

He was still in his suit, sitting in an armchair, when the phone rang. He knew what time it was for he had been awake listening to the radio – more mumbo jumbo about the re-construction of Iraq. It was 4.00 a.m., but he was not surprised to get a call. He was slow getting out of the chair and trod on his book as he made his way to the phone. He supposed it would be his son.

He recognised the voice of his daughter-in-law.

"I didn't wake you?"

"No, you didn't wake me."

"I'm glad. I don't want you to be sleeping when I'm not."

Before he could answer she had replaced the receiver. At last, blame had been apportioned. It was the first time she had spoken to him since the death of her son.

"Have a good time. Don't get your feet wet!"

She had been at the front door crying out as they left. He had driven over to collect the boy for an outing. They were going to the wild fowl sanctuary to take photographs. His grandson had a good eye and was patient. He could sit motionless in the reeds for an hour if necessary. It was odd really. In the house he was a fidget like most small boys, but at the lake he grew up. They were both competitive and had turned the trips into a contest. The game was that they each had five shots, taken in turns on the same camera. Back home, he transferred the pictures on to his computer and the boy's parents would later pick out the winner. More often than not, it was one of the boy's photographs that won.

The bird sanctuary was only fifteen miles away and even at the weekends the roads were rarely busy. They never hurried – the car was not up to it, for one thing, but more than that they valued the time they had to talk. Once at the lake, it would be hurried whispers and sign language.

That afternoon, he had a good tale to tell.

"What is it, Grandpa, what happened?"

"This is one of my true stories, alright?"

The boy had smiled.

"Well, you know how early I get up? This morning I went for the newspaper, same as usual, nobody around. On the way back, just after the hump-back bridge, where I start to slow down for the left-hand turn, that's where I saw it."

He had hesitated and looked across at the boy who had simply raised his eyebrows, old enough at eight to indulge a dramatic pause.

"It was a barn owl. It came up from the field and started flying alongside the car. I had the window down and the owl was no more than four feet from me at eye level. It was keeping pace with the car and, I promise you, it was staring at me all the way – as if I was a tasty field mouse."

He had been rewarded with a giggle.

"I was doing 20 miles per hour and he stayed with me for 200 yards, right until the turning, barely moving his wings to keep up."

There was more he could have said. He could have said it had felt like a blessing. That he had marvelled at the bird's face – in close-up even flatter than you imagine, like a cartoon bird that has flown into a wall. It had seemed a gift. Like the sighting of a kingfisher, a singling out, a portent of favour.

How wrong can a man be?

He made himself some coffee. There were already three full mugs on the draining board. They must have been there a long time, for a skin of dust had turned the black surface grey. He put the fresh cup alongside them and opened the back door into the garden. The night air was cold so he closed the door. Such is the banality of grief: the endless repetition of pointless activity. For two weeks he had walked the internal boundaries of his house, opening and closing windows, checking cupboards, peering into the empty fridge, climbing the stairs and wondering why. Even music had failed to bring relief. Every so often he would sit at the piano, but could never bring himself to play. Late in the day, fatigue would overcome his restlessness and force him into a chair, where he would sit waiting for sleep. Now with the confirmation of his guilt, that phase was over. He went back into the drawing room and took down the bottle of sleeping pills from the mantelpiece. Let's try oblivion, he thought.

He awoke hours later. His mouth was dry and his first conscious thought was of the boy and the sequence he was trying to erase from his head. Slowly the sound filtered through, a domestic duet of running water and the clink of dishes. Someone was downstairs. His front door was never locked. It had been a point of principle when he moved up from London, one of the reasons for coming. He had wanted to believe that what had happened to him in London had been a big city aberration; that here on the road to nowhere, the old certainties were still in place, that you could leave your house and car doors open and suffer no ill. He had been warned that it was no longer so and that his romanticism could be dangerous.

On the road to the lake they had pulled in at Barton's petrol station. It was one of the few independents left and its two pumps were seldom used. Locals and tourists alike preferred the facilities and lower prices of the Shell garage three miles on at the roundabout. Old man Barton had converted his redundant servicing bays into a mini-market and did a fair trade. It was a place where you could buy canned goods and jumbo packs of frozen chips, binding twine, shoe polish, a bag of coal, bread, newspapers and, in season, fruit, vegetables and flowers from the neighbouring farms and gardens. The produce was displayed on tables outside and there was usually someone looking it over.

It was part of their ritual to call in at Barton's for a bottle of chilled mineral water to take to the lake. The first time he had offered the boy a "swig" there had been a peal of laughter at the discovery of this new and disreputable-sounding word. Thereafter, it had been their name for bottled water.

"I'll get the swig."

He had jumped out of the car as he had done countless times before, leaving the door open and the engine running. Oh yes, and the camera case and tripod on the back seat. He winced at the memory. Later he had told the police that he had been aware of the young man at the tables, but had thought nothing of it.

He had been in the store perhaps a couple of

minutes. He would have been out sooner if Barton's married daughter had not sold him a raffle ticket when he went to pay. She had asked him to put his name and telephone number on the stub. Days later he had written it out again and timed himself. Fifteen seconds. It would not have made any difference. He could not blame her.

What happened while he was in the store he learned later from the young man's testimony. Lance Rivers was eighteen and addicted to heroin. He was hitching to his grandma's in Lincoln, the last member of his family prepared to give him house-room. He had pocketed some fruit from the table and was walking past the car when he had noticed the camera case. On impulse, he had jumped in and had been shocked to see the boy. He had yelled at him to get out and when the boy had opened the passenger door, he had slid across and shoved him hard, pulling the door to as the boy fell. Then he drove off. It was all a mad rush. He didn't know that the boy's foot had been caught up in the slack of the seat belt. He hadn't heard the screams in the forecourt – it was a noisy old engine. He didn't know that he was dragging the boy along the road at 50 miles per hour. He didn't know why the driver behind him was flashing his headlights, his horn blaring. He didn't know why a truck driver had forced him on to the verge at the roundabout. He didn't know why the newspapers were calling him a monster. He hadn't known the boy was there.

From inside the store he heard the car move off, the whining engine and clashing gears an overture of disaster. He ran to the entrance, fear turning his stomach, a sour vomit already in his throat. He threw open the door just in time to see the Land Rover leaving the forecourt in a cloud of black exhaust fumes. Through the haze he had seen the boy bouncing on the macadam. He was screaming "Grandpa!" – "Grandpa!"

He had chased after them screaming himself, God knows what – not words he thought, just a scream, a never-ending scream. He ran until his knee gave way. They had found him crawling along the side of the road.

Downstairs the noise had stopped. Someone must have looked in to help, probably his cleaning lady disregarding his instructions to stay away. Whoever it was had gone. It was safe to go down. The sleeping pills had made him thirsty and he cupped his hands under the kitchen tap and drank the cold water. When the phone rang, he answered it with wet hands.

"Dad . . ."

The receiver slipped from his grasp and smashed on to the stone slabs. He picked it up, but the signal had gone. When his son arrived with Beth twenty minutes later (the time it takes to drive cautiously from the one house to the other) he had found his father sitting on the kitchen floor, cradling the broken phone and quietly weeping.

PART TWO

LONDON

November 1999

By the time he finally left, the adulation was beginning to pall. There had been a month of farewells. Lunches every day, three dinners a week – all preceded or concluded with speeches and presentations. His clients had given him a gold pen; the staff, an antique watch, older than himself, but unlike himself, still burnished and bright. There had been photographs from his partners by names he revered: Doisneau, Bravo, Lartigue, all framed in oak, their certificates of authenticity housed modestly in brown manila envelopes. He was familiar with this trick of the rich, restraint adding to the value of the gifts, the generosity of the givers.

There were books, too, first editions of novels he loved – *Black Mischief* by Evelyn Waugh, published by Chapman and Hall in 1928 for 7/6, and now worth £400. They had found him a fine copy of Iris Murdoch's *The Nice and the Good* and presented it, he realised, with more than a touch of irony. There was a quince tree for his garden in London (to be lifted and planted at his command) and more than a hundred leaving cards and letters, many of great tenderness.

At the presentations he looked into his lap as clients and colleagues chronicled his thirty years in the company. Occasionally, he glanced up to acknowledge a common memory or to share in the enjoyment of his own edgy wit recalled from earlier days. On the Wednesday of his final week, the company had hosted the official goodbye in the ballroom of the hotel across the square. At 5.00, the staff meandered across the road, latecomers dodging the traffic in their haste to secure a good seat. It was the end of an era, they had been saying in the corridors. Even the graduate trainees who had joined the company just seven days earlier and had never actually met him were caught up in the conflicting emotions of the day: sadness at his going, gratitude for all that he had done, but also excitement at the prospect of change.

His three partners were eloquent, each generous with his praise. As he walked to the lectern to give his reply he was aware that everyone was standing. There was applause, a sea-roar in his ears, and he stood waiting for it to stop, smiling into the dark space above the heads of the audience.

In the pub later, the video team said it had been the longest ovation they had ever filmed. "Not that there was much to film, Henry standing there for five minutes and the rest just clapping their heads off. And that was before he'd even said anything."

He had worked hard on his speech. He knew they expected it to be the speech of a lifetime – quite literally the distillation of thirty years at the company, a list of do's and don'ts, a formula to keep things as they were – though in their hearts they must have known that was not possible, perhaps not even desirable. He knew it, too, and no longer wanted to make the speech of a leader. In the old days he would inspire them, lift their spirits and send them back to their desks with renewed energy and enthusiasm. Now he simply wanted to say goodbye and slip away. Somehow he had found the right words and if the audience missed the old fire they had responded to the gentle sincerity of his farewell.

On the Friday, the last day of a long week, Henry cleared his office. A tidy man on the surface, only he knew what chaos existed in the cupboards so exquisitely fronted with beech veneers and brushed aluminium. He threw out almost everything: letters, cards, documents and photographs. Crates had been sent up to take the books that lined one wall of his office. His books had been a daily comfort, confirming that even in commerce there was room for contemplation. Now he realised he no longer wanted them. He scribbled a note that they were to be given away. He left his awards, certificates and business degrees on the wall. He wondered if they would end up in the archives or the bin. It was all the same to him.

It was past 9.00 when he took the lift down to the basement. Even at that time on a Friday evening, the building was usually busy. In the meeting rooms, people would be working on presentations for the week to come. Often, they would be there all night – the conference tables littered with charts and the debris of take-away meals. When the cleaners came in at daybreak, they would sniff the air in reception, gauging the scale of the job ahead.

As the lift passed the fourth floor, Henry knew that Dan Priestly would still be at his desk – not working, but waiting. His evening routine was well established. First, *The Times* crossword and then television until it was time for the last train home to a wife he no longer loved. (A year later, in the Divorce Court, she would claim in all innocence that it had been the company's work ethic that had destroyed their marriage.)

There were many reasons for staying late and Henry was not surprised when the lift stopped at the second floor. A girl got in, someone he did not know. She was flustered to find him there. In the confusion he saw that she was tall with dark, cropped hair. She was wearing a long black coat.

"Ground?" he said. Before he could push the button the doors closed, leaving his finger redundant in mid-air.

She smiled.

"I'm Maude, one of the new graduates. I was really moved by your speech on Wednesday. I'm sorry we won't have overlapped for longer."

He said that he was sorry, too, and could think of nothing to add. He stood looking at his shoes until the lift doors opened on the ground floor. She got out. He felt he had let her down by failing to offer a suitable benediction. Well, he had no more wisdom left.

In the underground car park, his Mercedes stood alone, its black paintwork dulled by a light film of dust. For ten years he had grumbled about the fall-out from the cheap ceiling tiles, but nothing had been done. Now it did not matter. He drove up the ramp, only mildly irritated.

In the car, sensors picked up the first drops of rain on the windscreen and the wipers swept across the glass.

He is back again in California driving with Nessa and Tom to San Francisco. It is 1977. Tom is five and needs to pee. They are on the Seventeen-Mile Drive in Pebble Beach and there is no place to stop.

"You'll just have to hang on, Tom."

"I can't."

"Yes, you can. Just think of something else. It always works."

And then he pushes the windscreen washers so that two arcs of water rise and splash gently on the glass. He does it again and again.

"Just think about something else," he repeats. They are all laughing. In the front seat, Nessa grips his arm, "Stop it," she says, but her eyes are shining.

Reluctant to go home, on a whim, he drove to a small mews near Grosvenor Square. He parked in the shadows and turned off the lights. The rain was getting heavier. He looked across at the modest building where it had all begun. Management consultants had been less fashionable in 1970 and the investment in 1200 square feet of office space had seemed adventurous. He saw that an architect now occupied the first-floor offices above the row of lock-up garages. Today, the garages probably earned as much as the rooms above, but it had not always been so. He had been lucky in that building, winning his first major clients there.

He had always been fascinated by business, but he had never believed in making it more complicated than it was. He was suspicious of textbook managers, the graduates from business schools, who, fed on a curriculum of turbulent case histories, stormed out into the real world with an appetite for mayhem. He used to complain that they had been educated at drama school not business school. The people who had inspired Henry had been hands-on leaders who ran their companies the way they ran their lives. He admired patience and conviction and had found these qualities not in corporate time-servers, but in entrepreneurs, people who had put their houses and futures on the line to follow a dream. He had learned from them that, at its best, management was intuitive, honest and simple. He believed in common sense.

It was a belief that had brought his company early success. It had been one of the first in its sector to go public and had grown to become a group of twelve allied businesses encompassing everything from advertising to contract publishing. The original consultancy, however, had always been positioned at the centre of this wider universe – the place where the knowledge burned brightest.

Clients came to Henry for constructive, conservative advice: the rebuilding of assets, the freshening of known and traditional strengths, the protection and growth of brands. They went to others for step-change thinking, for remodelling on a giant scale with all the consequent upheavals. Such grandiose meddling had suited neither Henry's skills nor his temperament. He thought most change over-rated.

He slid further down into the seat as a car turned in to the mews. It stopped at a pub celebrated for its steaks. Three men were dropped off, bulky in their business suits and eager to get in out of the rain. Their voices carried.

"We'll be out by midnight."

"We may even be standing."

There was laughter and the car departed.

Thank God, his days of corporate entertaining were over. He had never been a comfortable host and after the Basil Hume evening he had given up trying.

The cardinal had been invited to speak at a black-tie dinner in a London hotel. Henry had reserved a table and taken a group of his clients. It was an all-male dining club with a simple code: total indiscretion inside the room, total discretion outside. The opportunity to let their hair down had lured many illustrious speakers to the club's evenings – even prime ministers – and it gave the members what Henry had come to see was their greatest thrill: the belief that they were in the know, right at the heart of things.

When Cardinal Hume rose to speak that evening, the room already greyed by the fog of a hundred cigars, no-one anticipated that he was about to give the most audacious speech in the club's history, more outrageous than anything they had heard from Thatcher, or Heath or Murdoch.

Hume had said very little. What he did say he said with his usual modesty. Perhaps he was on his feet for ten minutes. He told them to be good people and to do good things. He reminded them that they were leaders and that they had a responsibility to fashion the tone and conduct of their companies. He had spoken with grace and good humour, yet he had not tried to entertain them. He had sat down to restrained applause. The clients at Henry's table were barely polite. Naïve was the general verdict.

"If I want a sermon I go to church, not to Claridge's."

There was general agreement at the table, guests tapping their wine glasses with their coffee spoons to underline their approval of this sentiment. Henry said nothing. He had found himself moved by the cardinal's speech and admired its courage. He had resigned from the club a week later, pleading pressure of business. A meaningless gesture, since his partners went on taking the firm's clients to the dinners and Henry's absence went unnoticed.

Two young women came out of the pub arm in arm, their high heels barely coping with the slick cobbles as, bent double, they hurried to get out of the rain. Reaching the darkened car they stopped for breath or support – he wasn't sure which – their breasts flattened against the windows, their arms flung over the roof. They were celebrating an escape.

"Well, I don't have to put my tongue down his throat, just to say hello."

He lowered the passenger window and the car was suddenly full of curves and the smell of wet wool.

"What the fuck?"

They were startled, but when they saw him in the driving seat they ran off laughing.

He started the car and drove home, saddened by the empty seat beside him.

He lived just off the Fulham Road in a two-storey, double-fronted house that the local estate agent had sold him as "a country cottage in London". The house was larger than it looked, and in one of the three reception rooms there had been space to tuck his piano against the wall. He had taken lessons until the age of fifteen when hormones had directed his energies elsewhere. But on the death of his parents, he had claimed the piano and it had gone with him from flat to flat and house to house. It was the only remnant he had of his childhood, its tone a song line to his past. He played it late at night – hushed, tentative jazz – the chords barely reaching the walls.

His friends thought his house somewhat modest, considering his success, but Henry and Nessa had bought it for the gardens.

In the front they had planted four standard holly trees, each in a square bed of lavender edged with box. In the beds below the windows, catmint and lady's mantle were ground cover for Queen of the Night tulips in the spring and Japanese anemones in the autumn. The whole front of the house hosted a magnificent *Rosa banksiae* "Lutea" – small round buds appearing in late April, bright green and tipped with the yellow of the rose to come.

In the back garden, a formal pond took centre stage in a lawn framed by a mossy brick path. Behind this lawn, up two gentle steps and concealed for the most part by yew hedging, was a raised parterre and a small pavilion. Enclosing everything were walls of London Brick topped with lengths of trellis that buckled under the weight of ramblers. In summer, the serenity of the centre seemed always under threat from the chaos of the edge.

There were no lights on in the house when he arrived. He turned off the alarm and went into the kitchen. The morning's post was on the table, most of it junk. He sat down to open the rest, too tired to take off his overcoat. He had won £50 on his Premium Bonds. There was a brochure from a wine merchant, several bills and a letter erroneously addressed to Sir Henry Cage. He studied the envelope. The address had been typed on a computer, the label perfect – a secretary's mistake rather than a cynical ploy, he thought.

Having read the letter, he was not so sure. It was from someone he had met only once and instantly disliked. It appeared the man was now the chairman of an appeal fund for a government-backed business school. They had been awarded £30 million by the Lottery for a new building and needed to match that with a similar sum from the private sector. The letter said they were looking for fifteen key individuals who had an interest in business. In return for their £2 million they could have a scholarship or one of the lecture halls named after them. It was a crass letter, so inept that perhaps a title had been dangled, after all. He would not reply. He put the bills and the cheque aside and scooped up the rest for the bin. As he did so, he saw that he had missed one letter, an airmail blue envelope, the handwriting unmistakably Nessa's. He left it unopened on the table. He had not heard from her in five years. One more night would not make any difference.

2

In the village, they are known as part-time traders. In summer, when the weather is warm, they close the bookshop at lunchtime and cycle to the beach. In winter, they wait eagerly for the chill north wind that keeps people off the streets. On such days they bolt the door and retreat upstairs, consciences clear. From their bed of wrought iron and brass (restored for next to nothing by the book-loving blacksmith on a nearby estate) they watch the black clouds roll in from the North Sea. The clouds carry the rain south – south over their tiny roof, south over Garlic Wood and the cold Norfolk fields. The boy Hal lies snug in the big bed with them. They have been married for five years and despite some shadows in their lives, they have never been happier.

They are not as dilettante as the villagers imagine. Most of their business comes from their website and the catalogues they send out each quarter to a list of clients which steadily grows. They specialise in twentieth-century first editions, in particular, British and American fiction and poetry, an enthusiasm that Tom has inherited from his father. Summer visitors to the shop are dismayed by the metropolitan prices and the absence of beach books. More often than not, they leave empty-handed – a fact much discussed in the adjacent businesses. It is generally predicted that *Cage & Cage – Booksellers* will not survive. A video rental store is what most villagers would like to see as a replacement.

Large, serious, grey eyes gaze steadily at Tom.

"I need a bit of cold pillow, Daddy," he says moving his head on to a cool, unrumpled area. Tom is in thrall to his son, who is nearly four. Working from home, they have rarely been apart, so that now, when Hal goes three mornings a week to the village playgroup, Tom feels a lover's sense of separation. The boy is suddenly quiet – sleep coming with comic-book alacrity.

"Has he settled?" Jane says downstairs.

"Out for the count."

"You're going to miss him."

"What do you mean?"

"Well, he'll probably be asleep for ten hours."

"I'm not that bad."

"I didn't say it was bad."

Later, she looks up from the book she is reading, the new novel from a prize-winning writer they both admire.

"It's here. Page 32 – vertical sex – this time against a tree."

It was a game Jane played, spotting the sexual motifs in an author's work. Most writers of literary novels, she had found, repeated themselves; Updike, perhaps the most obvious exception, though latterly, even he had become predictable. She was not surprised by this erotic continuity. It is notoriously difficult to write convincing sex scenes and if a writer manages to pen one that does not provoke ridicule the temptation to use it again, with slight variations, must be immense.

"In his first book it was in a lift, in his second against a car and now it's upright in a forest – there's lichen on her thighs." She paused. "You know, I met him once."

"Oh? Where?"

"At a book signing in Norwich. Sadly, he was sitting down."

He grins. They were at a stage in their marriage when jealousy was not simply absent, but inconceivable. They still flirted with others at parties out of habit, but retreated if the returning banter was more than superficial. The child had made them inviolate. When Princess Diana complained that there were three people in her marriage, Jane had cooed to Hal, "And what's wrong with that?"

They had bought the shop with money left to Jane by her grandfather. What funds remained were for books not builders, so they had fixed the place up themselves. The shelving was not always true and there were imprints of their sneakers, like faint fossils, on the hastily painted floors. Sometimes as they worked she would look at Tom. What she saw was Tom repairing a door but, in fact, she knew that the work was repairing him. His parents' divorce had almost destroyed him. Now she, the bookshop, and Hal were slowly putting him back together again.

Tom is nine in the Polaroid, smiling by the pool in the Beverly Hills Hilton. He watches the print come to life, his skin darken to a tan. His father, holding the photograph, says, "I want you to look at this carefully, Tom." The boy leans closer, familiar with the magic of instant pictures, but happy to indulge his father with a show of wonder at the density of colour and the accuracy of the flesh tones. But his father does not want to talk about photography; instead he says, "I want you to take a good look at this because I never want to see you this fat again." Tom jumps back into the pool where the water will hide his tears. Does his father notice that he spends the rest of the holiday wrapped in a towel?

"Daddy, the soap doesn't work."

It is his twelfth birthday and he is getting washed and dressed, impatient to get down to his cards and presents. Henry walks into the bathroom.

"What do you mean it doesn't work?"

"There's no lather."

"Oh, come on, Tom, you've just got to rub harder."

"I've tried, really I have. I've tried for ages."

Henry comes to the sink. He takes the white bar and holds it to his nose. "This doesn't smell like soap, it smells like . . . like potato. You've been trying to wash with a potato, Tom."

He is chuckling and a slow grin breaks over Tom's face. It was a trick. His father had carved a fake bar of soap out of a potato and smeared it with lather. A joke before breakfast – was there ever a better way to start a birthday?

Fatherhood has made Tom uncertain. He can no longer

ignore Henry's existence. Hal's childhood unfolding in front of him revives memories of his own. And recollection blunts his anger. He is determined to be a father as unlike Henry as possible; calm where Henry was irritable; present where Henry was for the most part absent; tolerant where Henry was very often a nit-picking perfectionist. But then, somehow, the list breaks down. He cannot pretend that Henry had not been loving in the past. There had been happy times. He remembered a rented house on the six-mile beach at Hilton Head, South Carolina. The dawn walks – Henry, Nessa and Tom, arms intertwined, lurching in and out of the surf, sandpipers darting between their careless feet.

Memory makes him lenient. One day (but not yet) he will tell Henry that he has a grandson.

It is one of those mornings when global warming seems more seductive than catastrophic. It is mild enough for a walk on the beach before lunch at Jane's parents' house. They drive to Holkham, rehearsing the carols that Hal is learning for the playgroup's Christmas concert. He is insistent that alternate lines are sung "loud and soft" as Miss Martha wants. Nestling in the dunes, after the long walk out to the incoming waves and the seemingly longer walk back, Hal gets no further than "Twinkle, twinkle, little . . ." before he is asleep in Jane's arms.

Jane is twenty-eight, a tall, slightly stooping girl, sometimes beautiful, with hazel eyes and dark blonde hair. She listens with her body leaning forward. Her teeth are small and give her face an appealing (and deceptive) innocence. She is one of four daughters born to a Norfolk vet and his wife, and though she has herself no love for animals (the childhood rivals for her father's time and attention) she has found her lame dog in Tom.

She stands as he comes over the dune, hands full of shells for Hal.

"I didn't want to spoil your day," she says, handing him an envelope.

"There was a letter this morning, from Nessa. I'm afraid she's getting worse."

3

His paper-knife had been a parting gift from a grateful client. On the silver blade was the inscription "May I open naught but good news." Contrarily, Henry used the knife only when he anticipated trouble. He used it on all envelopes with clear windows; on everything from the Inland Revenue; on the stiff white envelopes that came from his lawyer and, now, on this unexpected letter from his ex-wife.

Nessa's handwriting, like everything else about her, was enthusiastic. Bold and inky, it whooshed across the page, letters almost tumbling over themselves in their haste to get the job done. This ebullience allowed her fewer words to the page, so she wrote as others telephoned – with economy. Henry once had been delighted to get a note from her at a dreary overseas conference they were attending together, "My door is ajar, and so am I," she had written. This letter, if less seductive, showed no change of style.

Dearest Henry,

I read that you have quit at fifty-eight. I'm surprised. I had you down for a lifer. Come and see me in Florida – in April – stay for as long

as you like. I want to talk to you.
Love, Nessa

The letter irritated Henry – its brisk tone adding insult to the injury he still felt. He resented Nessa's assumption that they were on visiting terms. He replied curtly that he was not sure of his plans and could make no commitment and signed it "Regards, Henry." (Having rejected "Love".) Petty, he knew.

In fact, Henry had no plans at all. He had arrived at Gate Retirement without itinerary, ticket or passport. In the days that followed, he would flit from book to piano, from piano to window. He could not concentrate on anything for more than a few minutes. When Mrs Abraham was in the house, he went for walks – walks that only increased his sense of dislocation.

"Hey, what you up to?"

He would turn to find someone at his heels on a mobile phone. London was full of people not wasting a moment and most of them, it seemed, had something to say. Everywhere, young people with big hearts and clipboards were waiting to accost him on behalf of cancer research, Alzheimer's, or starving babies. They placed themselves at twenty-yard intervals on busy streets and Henry found it impossible to run their gauntlet of goodness. Signing up, he felt anything but charitable. A mugging in a good cause still felt like a mugging. If it wasn't charities, it was time-shares or the *Big Issue* or a petition or a fake Gucci bag. He was living in a city of outstretched arms.

One morning, rounding a bend in Grosvenor Crescent he had found himself standing next to a motorcycle ablaze at the kerb – tidily parked, but shockingly alight, like a Tibetan suicide. He looked over his shoulder. The burning bike was outside the headquarters of the British Red Cross, but no-one had come out with aid. He went in and found a security man who eventually emerged with a fire extinguisher. There was just enough of the bike left to identify it as a Honda.

"What do you think happened?" Henry said.

"It's London, isn't it? Bloody madhouse."

Most afternoons, Henry was content to stay at home. Over the years, in addition to his photographs, he had built up a collection of twentieth-century British art, without ever owning a single first-rate painting. He had bought the works of Meninsky, Shephard and the like – artists with talent, but no great originality; painters who had needed to teach to pay the rent.

Henry was moved by their work. He admired their tenacity and was comfortable with their status. He viewed his walls with constant pleasure. He often said that he was surrounded by paintings that looked like the work of gifted relatives. He would have been uneasy living with art that was too obviously expensive. A Lucian Freud or Francis Bacon would have been impossible – like hanging your bank balance on the wall. In the same way, he could drive a Mercedes, but not a Bentley – live in Chelsea, but not Belgravia.

There were those who saw Henry's gradations as insincere, but his old friends were less cynical. Walter, his solicitor, and Oliver a friend since Cambridge, knew that Henry's dislike of pomp went back a long way. For the past thirty years, they had met every few weeks for dinner at a small Greek restaurant in Marylebone to discuss books, life and – in season – cricket. They had seen Henry poor and they had seen Henry rich, but they had never seen Henry overt.

After their most recent get-together, Walter had called him to check that he was alright.

"You seemed a bit down," he said.

Henry told himself he was wistful rather than sad. He listened to rainy afternoon jazz and the slow movements of symphonies. The empty days felt like the end of a love affair.

In quiet desperation he turned to old routines. Even when he was married, Henry would eat breakfast out of the house, stopping off at a brasserie on his way to work. Though he no longer had an office to go to, he decided to follow the same morning schedule. His breakfast companion had always been a book and for the most part he did read – though he also used the book as camouflage, turning the unread pages at suitable intervals as he listened in to neighbouring tables. (He had known for some time that a middle-aged man sitting alone with a book is virtually invisible.)

Most mornings he went to the brasserie in Sloane Square, which opened at 8.30 a.m. He usually arrived early and loitered in the entrance of the nearby tube station rather than join the queue and be marked out as lonely, unemployed or divorced. Though, as he ruefully admitted to himself, he was all three.

With time to spare, he had found himself lingering over breakfast – sometimes staying for an hour or more. He was aware that he was no longer just listening to the other customers, but often staring, too. Invariably, at women. He would, if challenged, have said that his observations were innocent enough – anthropological rather than predatory. For example, he had noticed that women on greeting each other always found something to admire in the other's appearance – "Oh that . . ." pointing to a necklace with a crude wooden daisy as its centrepiece – "that is adorable." In return, the daisy lady would find the scarf that her friend was wearing "divine, a fantastic colour".

Were they sincere? It seemed unlikely; though Henry was sure they were genuine in their wish to find something to like. Would the scarf lady have been pleased if her companion had removed the daisy necklace and offered it as a gift? He did not think so. Henry was confident that she did not actually like it. He had seen her reading a newspaper as she waited for her friend and it was clear that she still had 20:20 vision.

On the walk back to his house, the signs of Christmas were a daily depressant. For him it was a season of greater isolation and now, deprived of even office jollity, he felt a complete outsider. Three days before Christmas, according to plan, he fled. Since the divorce, Henry had spent the holiday in Barbados. He went back to the same suite, in the same hotel, year after year, flying in and leaving one week later. He knew nothing of the island apart from what could be glimpsed from the windows of the chilled car that took him from the airport to the hotel and back again.

His suitcase held few clothes, but was heavy with books. His great fear was of being stranded with nothing to read – so along with recent novels, he took bankers – books he knew he would enjoy reading again should the new titles disappoint. *Light Years* by James Salter always travelled with him and he invariably packed William Maxwell's *The Chateau*. Thus insured, even Christmas could be endured.

On the big night itself, he ordered room service and avoided the paper hats and festivities in the terraced restaurant. His room had a wrap-around veranda with shade and a view. It was on the top floor of a low-built plantation house that looked over the swimming pool. He was awake at 6.00 and would watch out for the early-morning swimmers and then shortly afterwards the chair-baggers with their territorial towels and paperbacks. In earlier, less affluent times, he would have been one of them, but now he was, quite literally, above such stratagems. He stayed on his deck all day, going down only for meals.

Guests were assigned tables on the terrace for the length of their stay. The positions, once negotiated, were guaranteed. The terrace, as is the way of these things, had its own Siberia and Golden Mile. In general, the tables around the dance floor were considered prime, under cover but close to the water. Henry, who preferred to sit at the back, had been greeted like a man who wants to pay full price at a clearance sale and had been escorted with much ceremony to a despised table. From there, he could watch his fellow guests, even if he could not always hear the quiet crooning of the nightly cabaret turn.

One night, Ken and Daphne, an English couple, paused at Henry's table to exchange greetings. Their recap of the day's weather had hardly started, before it was suddenly cut short. Henry followed their gaze across the floor and saw that their usual front-row table had been given to another couple.

"Oh dear," Daphne said. "We'd better see if we can sort it out."

He watched them go off to do battle at the captain's desk. Ken had twisted his ankle playing tennis and arrived at the desk, like a late-comer at an accident, envious of those that had been there from the start.

An inquest was in progress, apologies, a mistake had been made. The captain and four Barbadian waiters clustered around the couple. And then, above the chatter of the diners, above the soft lilt of the bandstand vocalist, came the echo of an older order, the voice of less egalitarian times, the throw-back tones of Ken – "Then why the fuck did you give the table away?"

"Ken, that's enough. Stop it, stop it, now!"

Daphne grabbed Ken's arm and pulled him off to an available table, one row back.

The singer went on singing, the waiters dispersed, no obvious signs of agitation, but harm had been done. Not to the waiters, whose calm indifference remained intact, but the rumpus had damaged Daphne. Her standing in the dining room had been undermined by Ken's tantrum. A recent graduate from the school of humiliation, himself, Henry admired her courage as she smiled and nodded at her new neighbours in the second row, but when the sommelier was dismissed by Ken with a sulky, "Same as usual" – it was one misdeed too many and she picked up her bag and left the room.

Henry recalled an airport, long ago. They had been returning from a holiday in Portugal and Nessa and Tom had been assigned seats twenty rows behind him. He had kicked up and made the girl at the check-in cry. Finally, they had been offered three seats together, but Nessa had refused to accept them. She had sat in the back of the plane with a baffled Tom.

He returned from Barbados on Thursday, the day before New Year's Eve. He had been asked to the big thrash at the Dome, but had made his excuses. Two of his clients were major sponsors and he had sat in on many planning meetings. He had not found them stimulating. The project had needed a presiding genius, a dictator. As it was, there were too many bosses, too many scared people running around trying not to give offence. Instead of the trip to Greenwich, he intended to spend the evening watching television and to be in bed by 11.00. He had long since stopped staying up to hear the chimes at midnight. Those nights were in the past: raucous evenings with friends in small Italian restaurants, bread rolls hurled from table to table, the wet kisses of unknown women as the clock struck midnight. And then out into the streets, Nessa, standing on the bonnet of a slow-moving car in the King's Road and mouthing words of love over the heads of the crowd.

There was a message on his answering machine. He was invited to watch the fireworks from a friend's riverside flat near Southwark Bridge. Nothing special, any time after eleven, bring a bottle.

He was fortunate to find a cabby on the King's Road willing to take him as near as possible to Upper Thames Street.

"Won't be easy, they've closed everything off. We'll have to go round the houses. Might be able to get you as far as Mansion House tube station?"

There were already thousands of people on the streets at 10.30, most of them walking towards the river. His cab headed north, against the tide, and on to the Marylebone Road. Here, the traffic was sparse and fast-flowing. Only at the traffic lights would you have known that it was a special night. Car windows were lowered as the habitual race to be first away was suspended and drivers found time to exchange greetings. A mini-bus drew up alongside Henry's cab. The passengers in the back were already merry and one of them dropped an empty whisky bottle out of the window.

"Happy fucking new century," they chanted.

Henry sank further into his seat, anxious not to catch anyone's eye.

The crowds thickened as they approached London Wall and the cab driver finally lost his sense of adventure. As he drove off, Henry remembered his umbrella on the back seat. Rain had been forecast for about midnight. He joined the throng walking purposefully towards the river. It was at this stage a silent march, everyone too earnest for talk, eager to get a clear view of the fireworks and the much heralded, but unimaginable, wall of fire.

The block of flats where his friends lived had been cordoned off by the police. It stood on a narrow alley leading to a short waterfront walkway. He explained that he had an invitation to one of the flats. "Lucky you," the policeman said, turning his back. Henry was wedged in by the crowd and could only wait for another policeman to come near enough to hear his plea. There was too much noise to shout. To his right, he could see kids climbing over the barriers and sauntering down to the river. The police, casually grouped around their portly motorcycles didn't seem to notice. "What about them?" Henry yelled, pointing to the grinning teenagers, certain now of ringside positions. A woman in a white, plastic mac tugged at his sleeve. "Don't worry, love, they're letting us all in at twenty to twelve."

"I'm sorry to be so late, they've only just opened the barriers."

"It's no problem – you're here, that's the main thing – and in time for the big bang, too."

Henry handed over his two bottles of champagne and received a full glass in return.

"Come and meet everyone. You'll know many of them."

William had been one of Henry's protégés, the brightest of the bright, and Henry's pick to run the company. Instead, William had decided to start up on his own. Failing to dissuade him, Henry had offered to back him, but William, wanting independence, had allowed him to take up just five per cent of the new company. It was enough; the two men, though separated by twenty-five years, were genuinely fond of each other and the business connection had added only spice to the friendship – the existing ties were already secure.

There were about fifteen people in the large interconnecting rooms and perhaps the same number of children, though it was difficult to do a head count of the young as they rushed from room to balcony and back again. There were several people from the company and he embraced them warmly. He saw Grace on the balcony and went out to greet her.

"Oh, you're here," she said, "I was worried about you. I know how much you hate humanity *en masse* – and, come and look – it's rarely more *en masse* than this."

She led him to the edge of the balcony. Looking down from the third floor, it was as if someone had lifted the lid of a tube train in the rush hour – people packed so tight that when the rain came later, it would fail to reach the ground.

"Have you seen the boys?"

"Yes, in passing."

He had been at Grace and William's wedding. He and Nessa were godparents of their eldest son and he knew, without a shadow of doubt, that Nessa would still be part of the boy's life.

"Quick, everyone on to the balcony. It's two minutes to midnight. Bring your glasses."

A short wait, almost silence, and then the air is rent with rockets, the grey barges disgorging their cargos with synchronised fury. Henry is reminded of newsreel footage of the Gulf War. The bangs are sharp, high on treble, and he would like to have given them a little more bass, but no-one else seems bothered. He sees that the adults are like children, their eyes bright and mouths agape, but the kids have moved on and are looking over the railings at the people below. The display lasts for sixteen minutes and is judged to have been wonderful. No-one sees the wall of fire. Half an hour later, pleading jetlag, Henry left.

He had been told that the underground station at St Paul's would be open, but he couldn't get close enough to find out. The crowds funnelled him against his will into Ludgate Hill and he decided that it was useless to resist. There seemed no alternative but to walk home. It had started raining, a moist, intrusive drizzle. In Fleet Street, the thousands walking west met the thousands walking east. He slowed to a shuffle. For a while, the crowds maintained their good humour. Parents with tired children in pushchairs took refuge in the shop doorways from the rain and the flood of pedestrians. He felt hot, distressed by the body heat of strangers pressed too close and the thick damp wool of his overcoat. As he approached the Aldwych, he stumbled but was kept on his feet by the press of the crowd. He started veering to the left. He wanted to get out of this rat run, to cross Waterloo Bridge and reach the safety of the south bank. Perversely, the bridge had been closed. It seemed crazy to channel people down the Strand towards Trafalgar Square. He stepped over a drunk lying in a bed of broken bottles, the blood on the jagged green glass uncomfortably vivid.

He kept close to the shop-fronts, hoping against hope that the alley by the Savoy had not been closed and that he could escape on to the Embankment. It was open. He sidled into its sanctuary. Fingers crossed, the multitudes would not follow.

The steps took him down to the rear of the hotel and he felt that the worst was over. The gate to the gardens was open and he took a short cut through the shrubbery. The rain had made the ground treacherous and he slipped, sliding down on to the pavement through a sea of mud. Someone helped him up. The crowds, if anything, were more solid than in the Strand. He felt like a foot soldier at the Somme; his fall had left his coat and shoes khaki with mud. Weary now, he joined the slow march to Westminster Bridge. His plan was to cross Parliament Square and then work his way to Belgravia and on to Chelsea. He looked at his watch. He had been walking for an hour and a half.

As he approached the bridge, youths made unattractive by drink and rain were dancing on a tawdry stage erected in the riverside gardens. The crowds here were impossible, like four football stadiums all letting out at the same time. Henry was frightened – fall now and he might be trampled to death. He started pushing towards the square. A man, just inches from his face said, "Don't bother, they've closed it, we've all got to go over the bridge." Henry turned round and was carried by a surge of the crowd into the back of a young man. The man elbowed him hard in the chest.

"Don't be silly, I can't help it – the crowd is pushing me."

The young man twisted to look at him. The crowd swept Henry forward again and he was tight up against the man's leather jacket. Henry felt a booted heel smash into his shin.

"Oh, don't be so infantile" – even as Henry said it, he knew it was the wrong word. The man lowered his head and brought it back hard against the bridge of Henry's nose. He slumped, head swimming, the pain acute, but he did not fall. The crowd held him upright. There was an illusion of toughness – the man they can't put down – and then a shift in the crowd and he was on the ground.

"Back off! Back off! Someone is down!"

He was dragged on to the pavement and propped against the balustrade. He was aware and embarrassed. People stepped over his outstretched legs, not always successfully. He was just another man who had partied too long, the blood on his face the legacy of a drunken fall. He got slowly to his feet and fumbled for a handkerchief. His forehead was bleeding, but his nose did not seem to be broken.

By keeping close to the railings, he made it across the bridge. South of the river the walking was easier. The crowds had thinned and he made good progress along the Albert Embankment. Oncoming pedestrians scuttled out of his way. Later, catching his reflection in a shop window, he understood why. His hair, thickened by rain and mud, was a wild halo above a soiled and bloody face. His clothes were dishevelled. He looked like a vagrant with a grudge.

He had expected to turn north at Lambeth Bridge,

but the police had erected yet another barrier. It seemed he had become a competitor in a monstrous obstacle race. He looked over the hurdles at the empty road stretching across the bridge, the first open space he had seen in hours.

"You'll have to go down to Vauxhall, that's the only way you'll get over the river." A man with a sleeping child heavy in his arms shrugged at the flat tones of the policeman. Henry wanted to ask why was the bridge closed – what logic from above had deemed it necessary to turn celebrants into refugees, to fuck up the first few hours of the new millennium? Newly cautious, he turned away. He did not imagine that policemen did head-butts, but decided not to risk it.

On Vauxhall Bridge he saw the first traffic. He was limping and his head hurt. There were still hundreds of people on the pavements and he walked in the gutter, too tired to cope with the minute changes of direction required up there beyond the kerb. When the gutter became too cluttered with debris, he stepped out into the road, ignoring the hoots of the cars and the insults of the drivers. He walked, head down, through Victoria and into Eaton Square. It was 3.30 in the morning and his ordeal was not over. On the Fulham Road, a boy and girl bumped into him. They looked no more than fifteen, cold and pinched in their T-shirts, clutching beer cans to their narrow chests. "Happy New Year," they shouted. Henry ploughed on, saying nothing, close to home now. They followed him. "Well, fuck you, you wanker. Fuck you!" A beer can hit him in the back as he reached his gate.

4

In Florida, it is hard to find a cautious property developer. Subsidised by the city managers, they fling up shopping malls at breakneck speed, indifferent to the fact that many of the ventures would never cover the city's costs. The Plaza Del Ray, however, had been a success; profitable for twenty years, it had only recently shown signs of decline.

The drugstore and the Italian restaurant had closed and only Jack's Café, with its white plastic tables grouped under the shade of the two large ficus trees, promised conviviality. True, there was sometimes a bustle inside Rita's Beauty Parlor – and the dry-cleaner's did a steady trade, pulling in drivers from Ocean Boulevard, but it wasn't enough to dispel the feeling that the Plaza Del Ray needed a face-lift.

For Nessa, the developer's plans had been invigorating. The ficus trees had been plucked out and were replaced by date palms, more in keeping with the Spanish colonial style the architects now desired. The flat, grey roof-tiles had been supplanted by tiles of chunky terracotta, ribbed and undulating. The plain walls were adorned with fake arches and capped with deep architraves.

Each morning at breakfast, Nessa watched the reconstruction work from one of Jack's tables now shaded only by the green parasols he had been forced to buy. The work was surprisingly simple; what appeared to be stucco on brick or concrete was, in fact, paint on polystyrene. Blocks of it, 2 foot square and 6 foot in length, were cut and moulded and then pinned to the walls. Two coats of acrylic wall-texture, the first in grey and then in sand, completed the illusion. The Plaza might now have all the integrity of a Hollywood film set, but new leases were being taken up and Phil, the drugstore owner, was coming back.

Jack welcomed this new vitality, but he mourned his trees. He had even considered selling up and going back to New York, but the life here was too comfortable to leave. He played tennis most mornings and in the warm Florida climate his sixty-year-old body got down to low balls on forty-year-old knees. For that alone, you stayed.

"You alright there, hon, you want a re-fill on that coffee?"

Arlene, the waitress with boyfriend troubles, sashayed round Jack and Nessa as they talked.

"So, when is he coming?"

"He's thinking about it. But he'll come – I don't think he's got much else to do."

"Does he know the way things are with you?"

"No, I'll tell him when he's here."

She stood up. "See you tomorrow, Jack."

He watched her go. They were both unattached and had become friendly when she had returned from England. With a little encouragement, he could have loved her, but she had sweetly deflected his advances and he had settled for what was on offer. They were best friends and dancing partners, nothing more, but that did not stop his pulse quickening every time he saw her.

Her house had been her mother's, the holiday home of Nessa's childhood. It was now the last modest dwelling on the Boulevard, a single-storey anachronism among the new-money mansions. From the road, it hunkered down in a hollow, so that only the green-tiled roof was visible from the gated entrance. At the back, a wooden deck faced due east. From the deck, a narrow lawn sloped down to the sea wall and the beach. Steps had been set into the wall and Nessa walked to the water's edge. Above her, cormorants cruised the shoreline. At her feet, sandpipers busily chased false leads. She had come here after the divorce and the ocean and the house had kept her sane.

She sat on the beach, her legs stretched out in front of her. She was proud of her legs; even now, she had escaped the river delta veining and cellulite of so many of her friends. Idly, she prodded the skin on her thigh. Scores of tight, parallel wrinkles appeared. Irrelevant though it was, it seemed she was just a finger-prod away from old age, her skin already half a size too large for her body. "Goddamn it," she cried and went back into the house, slamming the door so hard that the gulls decamped to a spot twenty yards down the beach.

She had been unlucky. Cancer of the womb is not uncommon and curable if caught early. The cancer usually begins in the lining of the uterus, the endometrium, and more often than not, it announces its presence, the most common symptoms being bleeding after menopause or irregular or heavy bleeding during the menopause. For Nessa, young at fifty to get this form of cancer, there had been no obvious warning, no red flag of danger. Other symptoms – the abdominal pains and the tightening of her waistband – she had not thought to be significant. Aware that her stomach was distended, she had put it down to ageing and over-eating. For a year she fought her tumour with low-calorie brownies, a story she told later with dry amusement.

The cancer had been high grade and aggressive and during Nessa's diet it moved deep into the wall of muscle around the uterus, then into the cervix and the lymph nodes in the pelvis, then on to the cavity of the abdomen before moving north for the lungs. She had endured surgery and regular bouts of chemotherapy, but three years later she knew she was not going to survive. She was out of remission. Her oncologist thought she might live for six months, a year at most.

Tom and Jane knew of her cancer from the beginning. She had sent a cheery, casual letter; it was a nuisance, she wrote, like an arm in plaster, inconvenient, but in time the body would mend itself and soon she would be as right as ever. Jane had replied: "It will be easier if we're honest, won't it?" and they had been.

Her cancer and her grandson had announced themselves at roughly the same time and Hal had always been her best kind of therapy. From the start they had been close. So confident and breezy with adults, she spoke at first only in whispers to Hal.

"Everything they have is straight from the store," she had said to Tom. "It's all unused, hearing and eyesight a hundred per cent – we grown-ups should keep the volume turned down." She was one of those people who instinctively squat to talk to small children and there was in her face a regularity they trusted.

Tom and Jane came for a month each spring and for another three weeks every other Christmas. In the summer she would visit Norfolk, staying for the whole of June. The generous month, she called it. A late spring and she was in time to see the froth of cow parsley in the lanes, while early warmth meant the old roses would be blooming in the grand gardens they visited. Whatever the prelude, in June the Norfolk countryside is rich with compensation. She loved this soft bounty and thought often of the garden she and Henry had created in London; apart from Tom, their most successful joint venture.

In Florida, it's different. What the English call gardening they call maintenance and the less there is of it the better. There are no flowers in Nessa's garden – she hated the gaudy colours of the busy Lizzies that line every driveway on the Boulevard. Instead, her garden is laid to grass, the tough, springy rye grass that can survive both sun and salt spray. She had worked hard to preserve the thirty inherited coconut palms that cluster around the house.

These trees used to be common in Florida, but they were almost wiped out by blight in the '70s. At one point, there were only sixteen thousand of them left in the state, down from seventy thousand in the 1930s. Nessa's trees, like most of the coco palms in West Palm Beach are given regular injections. The trees are still infected and if left untreated their fronds would turn yellow and die back, so every three months Nessa pays a man to give her palms their fix.

"I live in a place," she tells Tom, "where even the bloody trees are kept alive by injections."

5

The girl in the brasserie was having a row with the young man facing her. Henry could see only the back of the man, but he appeared the calmer of the two. She was angry, voicing loud words softly, denying them the volume they normally warrant – anxious not to attract attention. She was surprisingly beautiful.

In Henry's experience, rage is rarely an adornment. It might add colour to the cheeks and lustre to the eye, but these benefits are generally offset by the jutting of the jaw and an ugly twisting of the mouth. However, in this case, fury had done nothing to mar the picture. The girl looked magnificent.

A sudden movement interrupted his thoughts, chairs were being pushed back, the couple were on their feet; he realised with a sense of danger that they were changing places. The young man gave him a look before sitting down. There was something familiar about him, but there was no time to study the face. Henry had lowered his gaze and turned a page of his book, aware that he had been careless. Since New Year's Eve, he had been finding it difficult to concentrate. Even reading had failed to engage him. At weekends, he had become a regular visitor to the Round Pond in Kensington

Gardens, but he had been dismayed when the model-boat enthusiasts had started greeting him like a long lost friend. He thought of them as anoraks; forever pulling their boats in and out of the water, adjusting the rigging, tinkering with the control boxes. Their diligence seemed laughable. Did he really look as though he were ready to join them?

He knew he needed another holiday. His nose had healed, but he was sleeping badly. The random violence on Westminster Bridge had changed him. He had become a victim, and like all victims, expected to be a victim again. Walking the streets, he was often fearful, slipping his watch into a pocket when faced by crowds. Once he had taken an unwanted bus journey, simply to avoid a bullet-headed youth approaching him on the pavement.

Perhaps, he thought, he should accept Nessa's invitation and escape to Florida but that would mean letting Nessa back into his life and that required a magnanimity he did not yet feel.

It had not been difficult to trail Nessa. She had been researching a television documentary about the American space programme and usually worked in her study in the morning. After lunch she would leave the house and return at about six. In the evenings, if they were not going out, she worked, taking advantage of the time difference to talk to Americans in their offices. Henry never asked her how she spent the afternoons. Occasionally, there would be shopping bags in the hall or she would mention a friend's name or a film she had seen. It was true, too, that when he had been at the office he had rarely given her a second thought. They were not a couple who rang each other every day.

What had made him follow her? It had been so simple, so unlucky. From the back of a taxi, on his way home early from a client meeting, he had seen her walking in Walton Street. The traffic had slowed almost to a stop and Henry had his hand on the cab window, ready to open it and shout out, when he saw that she was smiling, looking straight ahead, walking and smiling.

That first afternoon, the first afternoon he had followed her, she walked from the house to an Edwardian block of flats overlooking playing fields, south of the King's Road. She turned into one of the doorways marked FLATS 36–49. He waited a few moments and crossed over to the door, hoping to find a reassuring name next to a doorbell – Gilly Webb, Amanda Norton or the Mammets, afternoon friends she had sometimes talked of. The entrance, however, could not have been more discreet. There were no bells or name-plates. Through the glass inner door, he could just make out a porter fussily squaring off a pile of magazines on a polished table. He retreated to a bench on the edge of the playing fields where he had a good view of the front door.

Nessa came out two hours later. Henry waited fifteen minutes and walked home. She was already there. Along the way she had managed to acquire a shopping bag from Gap.

"I was looking for something for Amanda's baby. Takes so long to find anything decent."

He followed her again the next afternoon. She was on autopilot; the same leisurely walk to the same destination. This time, Henry had brought a book, but had read only a few pages, when she came out, not alone. The man was tall, his dark hair cut short, almost shaven, and from the bounce of his walk, quite young. Henry followed them on to the King's Road. The man took Nessa's arm to steer her through the crowds. They were talking and the man inclined his head to catch her words. Henry was destroyed by their gravity.

Even before they got there, he knew they were going to the Chelsea Cinema. There is only one screen, so he could see on the board outside that the film ended at 6.10. At 6.30, he heard Nessa's key in the door.

"I thought we might see a film," he said.

"Oh."

"There's a new Woody Allen on at the Chelsea – we could just catch the 6.45 performance – do you fancy it?"

"Why not?" Nessa said, her coat half off, slowly backtracking.

Henry did not follow her again. There was nothing new to discover. It was just a matter of waiting. A week later as he was leaving for the office, Nessa opened her study door.

"Can we have a cup of coffee before you go?"

They sat at the kitchen table. She was calm and prepared.

"I saw you last week. Your book had a red cover and it caught my eye as we came out of the flat. I knew you had followed us to the cinema."

Henry grimaced.

"I'm sorry about that. It was cruel. The film wasn't good enough to see twice."

She looked up. "Do you think I saw it either time?"

"No, I suppose not."

"He's an actor, he did a commentary for me. I've been sleeping with him for three – no, it must be four months."

Her precision, her belated need for honesty, undid him. Head bowed, he held back the tears.

"Oh, come on Henry, don't get upset. It can stop. It doesn't mean very much. I don't really like him. It's not the end of us. Don't you want to know why I've been seeing him?"

"I'm not sure I do."

She left the room on tiptoe, as if in the presence of the sick. She closed the door quietly behind her and he heard the clatter of her accelerated feet on the staircase. She could not wait to be gone. The real nastiness came later.

6

For a few days Henry stayed away from the brasserie. He went instead to a new coffee bar on the King's Road, one of a chain much lauded by Tony Blair as an example of new-style enterprise. To Henry, familiar with the coffee-bar boom of the '60s, there was little new about it, apart from the queues.

It seemed to him that the bar had been deliberately designed to encourage delays. It was created for a generation that needs the endorsement of the herd – the familiar logo on the polo shirt, trainers with the right tick, nightclubs with reassuring lines. How else could you explain the faulty logistics of the place?

The design was too inefficient to be accidental. To screw up on this scale takes planning. Why else the single serving station and solitary cash-point? Why else the cluttered mix of eat-in and take-away? Why the eclectic list of coffee options? (Guaranteed to cause dithering.) Why the novice on the till at the busiest times?

It was the formula of a genius. How long before a newly elevated Lord Coffee was summoned to Westminster to head up the Prime Minister's latest task force on youth-focused enterprise?

Henry decided to breakfast again at the brasserie,

but to go half an hour later. There would be a different crowd at 9.00 and by then the angry girl and her boyfriend should have left. The new routine had started well. Leaving the house he had met the postman at the gate. It seemed a good omen. Simply by starting half an hour later he had already changed the shape of his day. He had his letters in his hand hours before he normally saw them. Perhaps he would have been happier as a late starter. If he had found time to have breakfast at home with Nessa, maybe he would not be divorced and worrying about a girl he had stared at in the brasserie.

She was there with her boyfriend at a corner table, both amicable today. It was busy and he had trouble finding somewhere to sit. He had seen them in one of the mirrors and hoped that they had not seen him. He found a table at the rear of the room and ordered a coffee and croissant.

One of his letters was from Simon Alders, a publishing friend, who wanted Henry to write a short ABC of management, the more personal the better. It was for a series that Henry was familiar with and he was surprised by the invitation. He had known Simon for years. As young men they had worked together as embarrassed trainees in the circulation department of a women's weekly. Henry had left to go into business and Simon to write a novel. His book, which had appeared two years later, had been a high-minded story about old age called *Remaindered*. Sadly, the title had proved prophetic and Simon had gone back into publishing.

Henry read the letter again. He wasn't at all sure that there were twenty-six meaningful things to say about management and he certainly was not going to prove it. He had always been wary of business books and their familiar lexicon of warrior virtues. At best, they take a normal business career with its usual mixture of talent, stupidity and luck and impose on it the neatness of post-rationalisation. The story is invariably one of unrelenting brilliance. At worst, the "wonderful me" quota is so generous that the books belong on the fiction shelves. He decided to send Simon a gracious letter and excuse himself.

A young woman had stopped at his table. Henry looked up to ask for the bill, but realised that she wasn't a waitress.

"I'm sorry to interrupt you. I'm Christine. I'm the manager – may I sit down?"

Instinctively, Henry reached to shake her hand. It felt cold.

"Look, I'm really sorry, but a customer has been complaining about you. He says you have been staring at his girlfriend – repeatedly – on several occasions."

Henry felt himself blushing.

"Is it true?"

"Yes, no . . . not really. If it's the person I think it is, I did look for too long about a week ago, I was thinking about something else and I just, you know . . . it was rude."

"He says you were staring at her this morning, using the mirrors."

"That's not true. I caught a glimpse of her in the mirror when I came in, that's all. That's why I came up this end of the room."

He looked down at the paper tablecloth, minutely aware of its coarse weave.

"There's no charge for your breakfast today – but it might be better if you went somewhere else in future."

"That hardly seems fair."

"I have noticed you before. Staring seems to be rather a habit."

Henry stood up and took his coat from the hook. He had stuck his scarf in one arm and could not get the coat on. She tried to help him, but he shrugged her off. "I'm alright, thank you." He gathered up his things from the table and rushed out, the hem of his coat trailing on the floor, an empty sleeve waving to the room. At the door he was delayed by a flurry of people coming in. He stood to one side, and looking back into the room had seen the couple watching him, the man throwing his head back in laughter. Henry knew then where he had seen him before – the man's moving head a chilling action replay. He was the man who had head-butted him on New Year's Eve.

On the last Friday in January, Mrs Abraham resigned.

Henry had stopped going out for breakfast and was often still in bed when she arrived. She was an orderly woman and her schedules did not allow for Henry's mid-morning presence in bedroom, bathroom and kitchen. Several times he had made her late for her afternoon job.

"To be honest, Mr Cage, it's not right – you moping around the house like this."

He had promised to be out of the house before she

arrived and to stay out until late morning – sometimes for longer. She had seemed unsure and before he knew it he had said, "Oh, and I'll be in America in April."

Mrs Abraham smiled. She routinely read the letters that Henry carelessly filed in the kitchen toast rack and had been waiting to learn the outcome of Nessa's invitation.

"Alright, we'll give it another go, shall we?"

7

It had taken Maude Singer six months and three interviews to get a job at Henry Cage & Partners and eight weeks to decide that it was not for her. Aged thirty, she had been the oldest person in that year's graduate intake, and that was the sole reason (though she did not know it) why she had been selected. It was Henry, a year earlier, who had begged that at least one of the next batch of trainees should have seen some life other than school, college and a gap year in Goa.

"Who do we get each year?" he had asked "More of the same – it's a very clever same, I grant you, they're smart and they do their homework. To be frank, they frighten me. They know more about our company than I do. What ever happened to careless youth? Where are the misfits, the scratchy bastards who are going to make us feel uncomfortable? Surely, we can take just one risk each year?"

And so Maude Singer who had been a ballet dancer until a knee injury had sent her home to Bristol and a belated History of Art degree, had been the company's one and only wild card in 1999. Why had she applied? She was not particularly interested in business, but she was intelligent, shrewd and tired of being hard up. She wanted a fast track to her own flat, a car, and money in the bank. Despite sending her C.V. to all eighty-four organisations identified by the Appointments Board at Bristol, only Henry Cage & Partners had been interested in a thirty-year-old with no commercial experience and a forty-page thesis on "The Sculpture of Frank Dobson".

There had been one other interview. A young banker languidly looking down her C.V. had stopped at the mention of her thesis, "Where on earth does he find the time?" he had asked. She realised he was thinking of a contemporary Frank Dobson, at that time the Health Minister in Mr Blair's docile Cabinet. She had answered leaning slightly forward in her chair, careful not to smile, "There's always a mallet and chisel in one of his red boxes. He does it whenever he can." The banker had apparently been satisfied with her explanation.

And now she had resigned. They had, of course, not let her go without the semblance of a fight.

"So tell me, Maude, what is this all about? We don't usually lose people this early in their career."

Ed Needy, director of personnel, was in his thirties. He was well built with a shaven head. His eyes were blue and gave a misleading impression of candour. He inclined his head a carefully calculated fifteen degrees off the perpendicular and gave her a steady look. A girlfriend had once told him that this sideways glance made her feel that he was looking into the wings of her soul and he now believed it a crucial part of his persona. Maude, thinking that perhaps he had dropped his napkin, looked down at the carpet.

“Don’t be embarrassed.”

“I’m not. I thought you’d dropped something.”

He had taken her to the Connaught Grill and they were sitting at his regular table in the window alcove. A trainee did not normally rate the £35 set lunch, but she was pretty and he feared that her departure would unsettle the other trainees.

“It just seems hasty, you know. It’s always confusing when you’re shadowing other people. Why not give it another six months? If you still don’t like it, well, that’s the time to leave.”

“I don’t think I can do that.”

He hesitated. “There’s nothing I should know is there? No unpleasantness, nobody making your life a misery?”

“No, there’s nothing. Everyone is sweet. There’s a great atmosphere, you should be proud. I just don’t like the work.”

He was tempted to ask her why she had applied in the first place and then remembered that he knew already. There were two envelopes in his pocket. One contained her P45 and a cheque for three months’ salary. He had decided not to let her work out her notice. (Why advertise the fact that his recruiting system was fallible?) In the other envelope was her initial letter to the company. He had intended to use it against her, but when he read it in the car on the way to the restaurant he saw that she had never been a gushing applicant. She had written that she had a good brain and that her career as a dancer had taught her discipline. She was eager to find out if these qualities would enable her to prosper as a management consultant.

He looked up from his grilled sole. "You've been working on the market appraisal for our French friends, haven't you? They want to get a foothold over here?"

"Yes, lights and fittings; mostly light bulbs, as far as I've been concerned. Lots of focus groups."

"Ah, I understand." His head had tilted once more. "You shouldn't judge us on those – how tedious they are – those front rooms in far-flung Basildon or Epsom – no-one telling the truth, perfectly dreadful, I know. But that's not the job, when these six months are over you need never go to another focus group in your life." It was all he could do not to lay his hand on hers and give it a reassuring caress.

"I know that."

She felt herself leaning to the side, mirroring his movements as some people unconsciously adopt a companion's accent.

"It's not the mechanics that are the problem; my unease is more fundamental. You see, I've discovered I don't care how many light bulbs the average householder buys each month and I'm sure I'd be the same with pension policies or water softeners. They're not things I want to worry about; I don't want them filling the space in my head. I don't want my highs and lows to be dependent on a Monday morning print-out from Asda."

She smiled at him. "I didn't know that before I started, but I do now. I'm sorry."

He had given her the cheque and told her that he wanted her to clear her desk that afternoon. He said it was company policy. But he had been nice and wished her luck.

"What will you do now?"

"Get a job, I don't know, wait table, see what happens."

She lived in a rented flat in north London in a street where every Edwardian house had been converted. The developers had found a way of turning wine into water, transforming large, elegant rooms into minuscule flats. What was once an impressive drawing room or master bedroom became a living area with kitchenette, bedroom and a shower/loo. That the bedroom lacked a window, that the dividing walls were so flimsy you could hear ice cubes tumble into a glass in the next room, none of that seemed to matter. The flats were sold or rented as soon as they became available. The road could no longer cope with the influx of more cars and residents. The bin men came twice a week, but there were always people who missed the collection and put their rubbish out late. Maude's street had become an all-night diner for stray dogs and urban foxes. The postmen had learned to deliver eyes-down, watchful for dog shit and plastic bags leaking trash. Double parking had become endemic and the hooting of trapped motorists a familiar refrain.

Maude had an attic conversion and counted herself lucky. There was a small sitting room with a galley kitchen, a bathroom, and best of all, a bedroom in the roof with a large skylight. She had placed a mattress on the floor directly under the skylight and on cloudless nights she lay there bathed in moonlight.

She had painted the walls and ceiling to resemble a woodland bower, treating the trees in the manner of

Mary Adshead, a noted muralist in the 1930s. Maude's degree in art history had refined her eye, but not her hand and her rag-rolled foliage had turned out more brassica than arboreal.

The only man who had stayed the night had laughed out loud on waking.

"I hope you didn't pay for that rag-rolling," he had said looking up.

"I did it myself."

"Look, I'll show you. Keep the movements tight and disciplined, see. Remember, always keep your circles small."

He was naked, bouncing unattractively on the mattress, using his scrunched up socks to demonstrate the correct technique. Maude had decided to follow his advice and ten minutes later had made her circle smaller by a factor of one.

8

It was Roy Greening who spotted Henry's letter in *The Times*. He read it with disbelief and ran chortling into the next office.

"Look at this, Henry has finally flipped."

Charles England looked up from his desk. "Read it to me. You look as though you'd enjoy a re-run."

"You'll enjoy it, too. Listen."

Dear Sir,

Like most Englishmen I am interested in the weather and am a regular viewer of the B.B.C. national weather forecasts. Am I alone in noticing that in a typical two-minute bulletin a disproportionate amount of time is allocated to Scottish weather? Understandably, Mr Fish and his colleagues are weather enthusiasts, and no doubt Scottish weather is richly varied and often more dramatic than ours, but that should not influence the shape of the bulletin. To devote half a forecast to weather of interest only to three shepherds and five fishermen (I exaggerate) while ten million of us in London are lumped together with the southeast and given a very few seconds is, I suggest, lopsided. True, we do have our own regional forecast, but, presumably, so too do the Scots. My question is: should not the weather that affects the most people be given the most airtime?

Henry Cage
London S.W.7.

"I rather think he's got a point," Charles said.

"Yes, but this is Henry Cage, ex corporate guru – what's he doing prattling on about the weather? It's so . . . it's so lightweight, don't you think?"

Charles continued to be tolerant.

"He's bored probably – and unhappy, too, I would guess. Have you seen him since he left?"

"Afraid not – miserable people make me miserable, too, so I avoid them."

"Maybe we should arrange a lunch?"

"He'd tell us to fuck off. Why should he forgive us? We took away his company."

Henry's removal from the business had been handled with firmness, if not with finesse. His partners had secured the votes of the two non-executive directors and had the support of the bank and key clients. It was suggested to Henry that he had lost his appetite for commerce and that some of his recent pronouncements at conferences and in the press (not to mention the Annual Reports) had been eccentrically anti-business and, frankly, unhelpful.

Charles had even tried to be philosophical.

"You, we, started this company because you believed there was a better way of doing business. And no-one can say you didn't practise what you preached. Most of the people in this building are sitting on comfortable nest eggs, solely because the partners distributed the equity so widely in the early days, though I admit there were some of us who, if allowed, would have kept more for ourselves." His attempt at humour was greeted with silence – his self-deprecation too obviously emollient.

"But times have changed. If I may say so, Henry, the kind of '60s liberalism that you believe in now feels antique. Legislation has made liberals of us all – minimum wage, equal pay, maternity, even paternity leave, the stake-holding society. The war is won, Henry, and yet you go on as though we were still at the barricades."

At this point Charles had abandoned any attempt at graciousness. "This has become tiresome to me personally – and counter-productive to the company commercially. For example, why shouldn't this company work for British American Tobacco? If we can help them diversify, make them less dependent on tobacco income, isn't that a good thing, not only for our shareholders but also for society?"

Henry had stopped listening. They were now on charted territory, the subject of countless board meetings. He knew that Charles would repeat the litany of business opportunities that he, Henry, had forced the company to forgo. It was true; in the short term, his righteousness had sometimes hurt the bottom line, but he had always been willing to play the long game. They, it seemed, were not.

They had offered him a more than generous

severance package, contingent on his going peaceably. He was at an age when he could retire without suspicion, they said. God knows, he had earned a few years in the sun. The minutes of the meeting would record only his decision to retire – irregular no doubt, but in a situation like this, the least his friends could do.

Henry had responded with a calm he did not feel.

"I accept, naturally, your invitation to leave. I regret that I no longer hold enough equity to influence that decision, but perhaps, even if I did, I would choose not to. You are right: I no longer belong here. I have never been more certain of it." He had paused and looked round the table. Only Charles met his eye.

"When the time comes, you can be assured that I will play my part in any sentimental leaving ceremonies you wish to organise."

He had stood up and left the room, his board file left open on the table. The silence was eventually broken by Roy Greening. "Well, he didn't seem to take it too badly."

Downstairs in the fifth-floor loo Henry was vomiting into a toilet bowl.

In fact, Roy had been wrong about Henry's letter. It had sparked off an exchange of views that had enlivened the letters page of *The Times* for three weeks. Nor had Henry been without support, the letters running 60/40 in his favour.

The B.B.C. had defended the bulletins. The time allotted to each region, they wrote, was dictated solely by the complexity of the weather conditions in that particular region on that particular day or hour. They did not monitor the amount of airtime allocated to each region, but they expected that if they did so, over the year, there would not be wide variances. They estimated that the extra staff hours involved in such a procedure would cost £20,000 a year, and asked was this really how Mr Cage wanted them to spend the licence money?

A stuffy response, Henry had thought and had said so when invited to debate the matter on *Newsnight*. He had been up against two defenders of the forecasts: a Scottish Nationalist M.P. who had thought the letter racist and a boffin from the Met. Office who had trotted out the official B.B.C. line. They had both been achingly serious. Henry had been rather flippant and he had left the studio in high spirits, pleased to be back in the limelight.

The euphoria lasted for two days. Friends had been on the phone congratulating him on his performance, even Mrs Abraham had been impressed to see him on the telly again. "Like old times, Mr Cage, and nice to see you spouting on about something that wasn't just business, if you know what I mean."

On the evening of the third day, as he was watching television with a supper tray on his lap, a brick was thrown through his drawing-room window. He cried out as the brick skidded across a table sending the framed photographs crashing to the floor. There was glass everywhere. His strangled cry became a bout of coughing, so it was a minute or so before he got to the door. Across the road, old Mr Pendry was out on his driveway.

"I heard the crash, saw a van driving away – sorry, didn't get the number, though – not with my old eyes. Play it pretty rough those weather boys." He closed his door, chuckling.

The police were sympathetic and gave Henry the number of someone who would board up his window. They were honest enough to admit that the chances of identifying the culprit were zero, unless he or she did it again and got careless. They promised to make sure a police car patrolled the street for the next few evenings. "Chances are it was a random piece of hooliganism. It could just as easily have been the house next door."

It was not, however, the house next door that had dog turds posted through the letterbox that weekend and it was not next door's front garden that was doused with industrial bleach the following Tuesday night. The police conceded that the vandalism was targeted and extended the evening patrols, but short of mounting a 24-hour guard outside Henry's house (not possible with their reduced resources) there was little else they could do. It was suggested that Henry might like to hire a private security firm – the implication being that he could afford it.

"Saw you on the box the other night, sir. Nice suit."

So far, life had never given Henry the chance to find out if he was brave. He had been a child during World War II and had kept his satchel on long enough to escape National Service and the skirmishes of the '50s. At school he had avoided violence, was always adept at talking his way out of trouble. He was nervous of heights, but that did not necessarily make him a coward, though he suspected that he might be. When the runaway horse threatened to flatten the child, would he spring forward and scoop the infant up in his arms, or would he be transfixed, too petrified to act? Why does one man's adrenaline go to his legs and another's to his fists? Faced with danger, would he be a runner or a fighter?

Once, at Cambridge, Henry had been involved in a nocturnal prank when, for a bet, he and a group of friends had climbed into a neighbouring college to steal their first eight's oars from the Porter's Lodge. They had been blacked up, and tanked up, too, but they did manage to remove the oars, and later deliver a juvenile ransom note to the Warden. But what Henry remembered most clearly of that night had happened earlier.

They had been crossing the main quad, commando-style, running low, one at a time, across the lawn into the safe shadows of the cloister. The last of them had just made his ground when a triangle of light spilled out on to the grass – a porter had come out of one of the staircases for a smoke. Henry had hidden behind a pillar, his heavy torch poised to hit the porter if necessary. It would have been a gross over-reaction. Even now he shuddered to think what might have happened had he felled the poor man. Henry would certainly have been sent down; he might well have gone to prison. Yet in the heat of the moment he had been tempted. It would not have been courageous. The porter had been armed only with a Woodbine and Henry had been in no danger. What would he do now if confronted by the vandal? He had no idea.

The night after the police stopped their patrols, Henry's car was vandalised. A can of white paint had been emptied on to the bonnet of his Mercedes. It made no sense. A few days later, Henry received a letter. Inside the envelope on a single sheet of paper someone had scrawled the letter P with a blue felt-tip pen. The postmark showed that the letter had been posted in Clerkenwell. The following day another envelope came, postmarked S.E.3., with the letter E inside. By the third day and the arrival of the letter R (posted in Hampstead) Henry had a good idea where the correspondence was heading. The next letter, again posted in a different part of London, confirmed his suspicion; someone not short of first-class stamps was calling him a pervert.

"I've found with this kind of muck, sir, the victim often has an idea who might be sending it; I mean, pervert is a pretty specific kind of insult – you know, there's usually some incident that gives us a lead. You're sure you can't remember any sort of unpleasantness?"

"No, I'm afraid not."

Henry had never been a convincing liar and the detective sergeant did little to disguise his scepticism.

"See, my theory is: someone saw you on the television and was able to put a name to your face and then track you down."

"I'm ex-directory."

"But Henry Cage & Partners isn't, is it? I rang them

– pretended to be a friend from New York who wanted to send you a book. They gave me your home address right off. And I don't even have a good American accent."

Henry had not wanted to tell him about the head-butting and the incident in the brasserie. He sensed that the detective already half believed that the letters must have been justified. No-one is called a pervert without reason. It's not like "Rich bastard" or "Wog". It's not just a piece of name-calling, there's a narrative attached to it, there's a story there somewhere.

"I'm sorry, I can't think of anything. I'll ring you if I do." Henry had wanted him out of the house.

"You won't do anything stupid? No go-it-alone stuff?"

Henry played a straight bat.

"Since I don't know who to go for, that would be difficult."

9

The vandalism had made Mrs Abraham bellicose and Henry had found her constant suggestions tiresome.

"What about security lighting, Mr Cage? They say it really cuts down crime. Floodlight the front of the house. That's what I'd do if I had the money."

"Well, let's see, shall we? Maybe whoever it was is finished now."

She sniffed. "Why should they stop? Nobody's doing anything to make them stop."

Henry had noticed that she spent a lot of time cleaning the front windows or sweeping the front path. He suspected that she was checking all traffic, both vehicular and pedestrian.

"Housekeeper Makes Citizen's Arrest" – he imagined the headline and a photograph of Mrs Abraham at the front door, looking so very much at home.

He had invited her to take two weeks off with pay until things got back to normal. He had said he thought he might go and stay with friends and get some sleep. She had accepted her unexpected break with good humour, sensing the lie, but letting it pass without challenge.

As soon as he had the house to himself, Henry

became nocturnal. There had been no more letters and the past few nights had been uneventful, but he knew that it was not over – he felt sure there was more to come. He sat up all night in a drawing-room chair pulled up to the window. There was no street lighting immediately outside his house, but he could see the gate and the white picket fence well enough and the road beyond.

When he grew weary, he listened to the 24-hour news on a radio small enough to nestle in the top pocket of his jacket. He had bought it to take to Test Matches, but for the past year had been taking it to bed. It was the only way he could get to sleep. He lay on his right side, an earpiece in his left ear and he would drift off as reports came in of rogue kangaroos terrorising a small outpost in Northern Australia or of a totally tattooed man in Alabama. There is not enough real news to fill twenty-four hours and by 4.00 in the morning trivia is rampant. It is easy for the brain to close down in self-defence, but now the same banality and repetition had to keep him awake.

He had a large thermos of black coffee beside him and sandwiches bought earlier in the day. Anxious not to reveal his presence at the window, he had removed the sandwich wrappings in the kitchen to keep the noise down. He was aware that he was being ridiculous.

The first night he had managed to stay awake. He had even enjoyed the experience. His street had once been a rat-run connecting the Fulham and Brompton Roads, but pressure from the influential residents association had persuaded the authorities to make the street one-way and now it was of interest only to residents, tradesmen, the relevant utilities – and (at least) one vandal.

By midnight the social comings and goings were over, the Wilkinsons a conspicuous exception. They had arrived home at 1.30 a.m. in their Lexus 400 – a car shaped much like themselves – too heavy in the front to be graceful. They had slammed the car doors with tipsy abandon and then with fingers to their lips had hushed each other to their front door.

At 2.55, the clouds had parted and moonlight glossed the roof tiles of the houses opposite. Mr Pendry had paid a visit to the bathroom at 4.15 and a black cat had daintily walked the length of Henry's garden fence shortly before 6.00, when the *Today Programme* had rescued him from the inanities of all-night news. He had gone to bed at 7.00 but found it impossible to sleep. Daylight seeped in through the curtains and he was conscious of the sounds of the day beginning; the rattle of the letterbox as the newspapers arrived, the bleep of a reversing dustcart, the squeak of next-door's gate. After an hour, he went downstairs and retrieved his radio, finally falling asleep to the estuary tones of a phone-in.

That afternoon he walked to the Conran Shop to buy a torch. He had once sat next to a woman at the Royal Opera House who had the score of *Tosca* opened on her lap. Before the performance began she had turned to him. "I have this torch that doesn't spill light. I don't think it will bother you." She had been right, and now he thought such a torch would be useful; he could read or write without revealing his presence in the window. Better still, there would be no need to turn on his radio.

He took up his position in the window shortly after midnight. He had watched television most of the evening in his study at the back of the house. He had received one phone call. Detective Sergeant Cummings rang to see if there had been any developments.

"No, everything's been pretty quiet."

"No more letters?"

"Not from him."

"Oh, so you think it's a man, do you? Any reason for that?"

Henry had recovered, not well, but quickly.

"Sorry, I'm of that generation that automatically thinks all doctors, judges and taxi drivers are male. Criminals, too."

The detective had paused before replying.

"Alright, Mr Cage, let me know if anything happens."

If anything had happened that night Henry would not have been awake to see it. He had drifted off shortly before 1.00. Waking at 7.00 he had gone outside to check the front of the house. Nothing seemed to have been disturbed. Inside, he inspected every room, opening wardrobes and cupboards, needing to know that he was safe. It reminded him of a ritual that had marked him out at boarding school. A homesick eight-year-old, he would not get into bed without patting the bedspread first to make sure that no upturned dagger awaited him.

In the ruthless community of the dormitory he had been subjected to nightly ridicule, each boy elaborately patting beds, curtains, floorboards and chairs in search of hidden danger. The ragging had gone on for weeks, until one night, exhausted by a cross-country run, Henry had fallen straight into bed, too tired to be timid. He had never patted the bed again and yet even in adulthood some residual anxiety remained. Nessa had teased him about keeping a baseball bat in the bedroom and here he was fearfully opening cupboards in a locked and alarmed house.

The following day had been like a day of jet lag. In the morning, he had mooned about the house, watchful and weary. He needed regular hours. He wanted to sleep in the dark and wake with the light. He decided to sit up for just one more night. By the afternoon, fatigue had blunted his instincts and he allowed himself to believe his troubles were over, that he had been mistaken, that the malice had been haphazard and would pass on. Sitting in the window that night he became almost light-hearted with relief. Listening to the radio, he dispensed with the earpieces and curled up in the chair, his head cushioned on the soft and ample arm. It was a position, he knew, likely to send him to sleep, but so what?

He awoke to the sound of the newspapers being delivered. But was it not too early? There was something wrong. His watch had twisted around on his wrist and he was confused and looked for it in the folds of the chair. It was barely light outside and someone was knocking on the window. Henry could see white knuckles rapping on the glass and the cuff of a black leather coat. When he stood up his knee locked and by the time he got to the window he saw only the gate swinging back into place. He sat back on the chair and took a sip of coffee straight from the flask, scalding the roof of his mouth. Why had he come – what had he done? The click of the letterbox replayed in Henry's ear. The bastard had put something through the door.

In the hall he expected to see more dog shit, a firework or worse, but on the mat there was a plain buff-coloured envelope. He picked it up and carried it into the kitchen. The envelope was about five inches by seven inches and felt light. It could not contain more than a few sheets of paper. He tried to recall what he had read about letter bombs. He thought they had to be bulkier than this, more like a package. He took a knife from the dresser drawer and opened the envelope. Inside, a sheet of paper was folded around three Polaroid photographs, all variations on a single theme. He recognised the girl immediately: she was the head-butter's girlfriend, naked on a bed, smiling into the lens, knees spread, her hands easing back the lips of her vagina. Two of the pictures were close-ups.

10

Tom watched her plunge the massed tulips straight into the vase, never doubting that they would assume the right collective shape. As she leaned forward, the corn of her hair mingled with the tight green sheaths. It seemed to him that she was incapable of acting without grace.

"I'm thinking of getting in touch with my father."

She stood back from the table, looking at the flowers.

"Does Nessa want you to?"

"She's invited him to Florida – when we're there."

"Then I guess she does."

At lunchtime he collected Hal from school. They walked home on the marsh path behind the cottages that line the narrow main street. If they looked to the left they saw the backs of the houses – sheds and outbuildings bundled close to the back walls for comfort. On this coastline the wind blows uninterrupted from the Arctic Circle and smacks hard into the shore. Dotted here and there are hidden yards, revealed only by the high cab of a truck or the mast of a dinghy protruding above the brick and flint walls. Closest to the path are the allotments. Some of the lines still offered up cabbages, but most of the soil was tilled and tidied for the winter.

Turning to the sea, they lowered their heads, for the gale blowing across the marshes was too raw to look into. Heads down, they raced each other home, Tom careful to let Hal win, but only just.

In the afternoon, Jane took Hal to her parents' house. Her father had been given permission to fell a strand of poplars on his land. Years ago the trees had been a cash crop: Bryant & May, eager buyers of the timber for matches. Now that trade had gone and the wood was used only to make pallets. An inglorious end, in Jane's opinion, for such wonderful trees. There was a time as a young girl when she had started each day by calling out a greeting to the poplars from her bedroom window. In spring, the leaves are barely green and delicate enough to catch the lightest breeze. At twelve, she had described them in her diary as waving to her from across the fields. When her father had told her it was time for the poplars to come down her eyes had filled with tears and they had argued. Now, she had taken an excited Hal to watch the trees fall. Was it to please her son or to placate her father?

Tom knew it was neither. She was there for the same reason she would get up at 5.00 in the morning to see a friend off at the airport. She believed in leave-takings – in saying goodbye in person.

With the house to himself, Tom went down and closed the shop. It was too bleak a day for customers. In the back office, books were stacked on the table awaiting despatch. He was tempted to spend the afternoon with brown paper, bubble-wrap and tape – anything to put off writing to his father. He tried to map out a letter in his mind, a chronological survey of their estrangement, but it seemed stale news, so long ago.

His mother's lover had been famous: the male lead in a television soap opera, playing a charismatic, but chancy womaniser. When the actor's life coalesced with that of his character, the tabloids couldn't resist. "TERRY STEALS TOFF'S WIFE" was the front-page headline in one of them. Below was a picture of a harassed Henry outside his house. Photographers had camped by the garden gate for days. Who had tipped off the press? Tom remembered that his father had suspected the actor himself and later events had, perhaps, proved him right.

Three months later the affair was over and Hugh, alias Terry, had moved on to the young, blonde presenter of a regional breakfast show. The newspapers had been merciless. The following week Nessa had been photographed in her local supermarket buying what the caption gleefully described as "dinner for one". That morning she had rung Henry wanting to return, but he had refused to take her back.

"I can't. I just can't."

"Fuck it, Dad, she needs you – she's falling apart. What's the point of being so bleeding saintly at work and a bastard at home? For God's sake, help her."

Tom's voice had tailed off, so he was never sure if his father had heard his final coda, "Help *me*."

This Court of Appeal had been held in Henry's office. He had been determined not to let the newspapers disturb the workings of Henry Cage & Partners and had arrived at his usual hour. The photograph, cruel as it was for Nessa, was for him only the latest in a long series of public humiliations. The loss of wife had been a one-off misfortune; the loss of face seemed to be never-ending.

The post room had not circulated the red-top papers that morning, but by 10.00, even those locked in early morning meetings, had seen the picture of the boss' wife getting hers at the chilled foods cabinet.

"I can't do it, Tom. I'm sorry."

He had picked up the telephone on his desk and started talking to his secretary in the outer office.

Tom had gone back to Norwich, taking Nessa with him. He was in his last year at university and sharing a flat with Jane. He knew that Nessa should not be alone. Of the two rejections it had been Henry's that had inflicted the most damage. She was still Nessa, gamely talking of a new life and no regrets, but her body gave the lie. She had lost eighteen pounds and her limbs were never at rest, her legs jigging constantly as she lay on the sofa.

Tom and Jane were in the middle of exams and out for most of the day at the university campus. When they returned in the evening, Nessa was invariably stretched out on the sofa, often asleep, a book – and sometimes a bottle – open on the floor beside her.

One night Jane had found her sitting up at 3.00, ankle-deep in family photographs. Her legs were twitching so violently that the prints would not stay on her lap.

"Shit, I can't seem to keep my legs still. You don't have any diver's boots, do you?"

"Hey, it's alright."

They had clung together.

"What a mess. I miss him so much."

Jane held her hand, waiting for the sobs to end.

"You know, when I was with him, I often wished he were different. Now I just wish he were here."

"How do you mean, different?"

Nessa took a handful of tissues from the pocket of her dressing gown and pressed them to her eyes.

"More careless, I suppose. Someone who wasn't always quoting the latest health scare in the newspapers; I longed for some loose and cheery man who didn't ever so slightly narrow his eyes when I reached for a third glass of wine or ordered chocolate dessert in a restaurant."

She returned to the sofa.

"Henry was never much good at enjoying himself. He was always giving things up – wine, sugar, caffeine . . . and finally little old me."

"You did give him some encouragement," Jane said.

"That's true." Nessa turned her face into the cushions. Soon she was breathing heavily, even in sleep her legs moving to the miserable beat of her heart.

She had stayed with them for a month. Finding herself unrecognised, she had started going out. First, just on errands, but then for long walks through Norwich. She put on weight and gradually regained control of her body. When the exams were over they rented a car and drove north each day to the coast and it was there, lying in the sand dunes under a wide blue sky that she had told them of her decision to return to the house in Florida.

Dear Dad,

He touched the return key eight times and cleared the screen. He had always called his father "Dad" – but now it felt too affectionate, too forgiving. He started again. He had decided to be brisk.

Dear Henry,

I read of your retirement – congratulations, if they're in order. I can't imagine how you spend your days without the office, though I understand you're going to be spending some of them with Nessa – which is why I'm writing. We are likely to be there at the same time and I thought it would be less awkward for Nessa if we had at least met before then. Would you come to lunch one weekend? If you would like to, please get in touch.

He had printed it out on bookshop notepaper and signed it simply "Tom". It was already dark when he went out to post the letter. On her way home, Jane had caught him in her headlights, his giant shadow thrown on to the side of a house like some proletarian hero in a Soviet mural. A man, letter in hand, heroically confronting the future.

11

With Mrs Abraham away for another week it was safe to keep the Polaroids close to hand, tucked amongst the bills in the toast rack. He looked at them three or four times a day. He knew they had been delivered to taunt him, gloating proof of the young man's access to flesh he imagined coveted by Henry. The head-butter's youthful assumption was trite, but understandable.

It had been a summer's day in 1959. He had been standing in the middle of the Goldhawk Road, his arm around a girlfriend's waist, when a dark green Jaguar XK150 convertible had stopped beside them. The driver was waiting in a line of traffic before turning left into Lime Grove, at the time the London home of B.B.C. Television.

The car's top was down and he had recognised the driver, a veteran journalist who had found fame as the presenter of a current affairs programme. Henry was admiring the car when he noticed that "Mr TV" was checking out a different kind of bodywork. His interest in Henry's girlfriend had been so brazen, that Henry had called out, "Forget it – you're way too old."

His spite had been lost in the traffic's din. The

presenter had proceeded serenely to the studio where Henry had imagined him joking with the make-up girl about the joys of summer, the flimsy frocks, and the cracker he had just seen crossing the road.

Oh yes, Henry understood the head-butter's disgust well enough, but in this case it was unjustified. Henry did not see himself as some sad, old lecher. It had been the girl's suppressed rage that had first attracted his attention, not her body, though it was obvious from the photographs that her body was gorgeous.

The day before Mrs Abraham's return, Henry went to the glass-fronted bookcase in the drawing room and slipped the Polaroids between the pages of a book. He decided to keep the volume on the top shelf and had put it there with all the circumspection of a law-abiding newsagent.

The next morning he was out early before Mrs Abraham arrived. He had decided to do what he should have done a long time ago – sit down and talk to the head-butter, man to man.

Henry was not used to people disliking him. He had sauntered through life in the glow of easy approval. The incident on Westminster Bridge had not only been an affray, it had been an affront. The instant aggression and then the viciousness of the subsequent persecution had perplexed him. He worried that luck was deserting him. First, there had been the split with Nessa and Tom, then the loss of the company and now this. Well, this, at least, he could deal with.

Confronting the head-butter meant going again to Sloane Square for breakfast. He was gambling that the manageress would not be there. She might even have moved on, the staff were always changing. He did not believe that she would have issued an alert about him. It had been, after all, a minor matter, not really an offence at all.

He was on the doorstep at 8.27, perfect timing to get one of the two window tables in the non-smoking section. A quick look round revealed that neither of his antagonists were there. He ordered a coffee and croissant and opened his book, prepared to wait.

Someone was standing by the seat opposite to him. Without lifting his head he was aware of the black waistcoat and white apron of one of the waitresses. Oh God, he was going to be asked to leave. His description was probably pinned on the staff notice board: "*Public Pervert No.1. Well-dressed man (suit) in his fifties, dark hair, tall – usually operates with a book as camouflage.*"

"It is you, isn't it?"

"Yes, I suppose it is." He closed his book. "Don't worry, I'm just going."

He was not sure if free breakfasts were standard with every eviction and not wishing to appear presumptuous, he added, "I'll need a bill, if you don't mind."

"You are Henry Cage, aren't you?" The voice was friendly. "You don't remember me?"

He looked at her for the first time. Short dark hair, lively eyes, a nose without a trace of pertness. She could have been a refugee from one of his Lartigue photographs, a Bibi or a Renée. On the slopes at Megève or through the windscreen of a Bugatti, he surely would have recognised her, but here . . .

"I'm sorry."

"I worked at your company. We met in the lift on your last day. I was one of the new graduate trainees. Maude Singer."

She held out her hand. He shook it with a smile of relief.

"As I remember, I was rather tongue-tied."

"No, I was gushing. Silence was the most appropriate reaction."

"What are you doing here?"

"About to get fired if I don't get back to work – and no, I didn't get the sack from Henry Cage & Partners – I left of my own accord."

"I'd like to hear why."

She shrugged and was gone. Henry eked out his coffee for another twenty minutes but there was no sign of the head-butter. He paid the bill and left. At the door, he looked for Maude but did not see her.

On his way to breakfast the next morning, Henry found himself humming. It was like rediscovering a former, happier self. In the office, in the good old days, he had often startled colleagues by humming to himself in meetings. He hummed as others might pull reflectively on an ear lobe.

Once, while making love to Nessa, he had inadvertently hummed a few stanzas from "Waltz for Debby", an old Bill Evans piano piece that they both liked. Not surprisingly, she had pitched him off the bed. Later, she had said she might have stayed put for the whole track, it was after all a nice slow beat, but she had known that

Evans had dedicated the work to his three-year-old niece.

"It just didn't seem right," she had said to a laughing Henry.

12

That morning Jack had entered his café without opening the door. The glass panel had been smashed in during the night and Jack had charged through the gap as though the thief might still be there, his shoulders brushing glass from the door frame. The till had been lifted from the counter and thrown on to the floor and now lay on its side, the cash drawer open and empty. The glazing he could get fixed for a couple of hundred dollars, but the till was a nuisance. And all for thirty bucks, the small float he left in the till each night for the following day.

"Jesus, the jerk didn't even know how to open a till – you push a button, not chuck the bloody thing on the floor."

"Even thieves aren't what they used to be."

There were four of them sitting round the table: Jack, Hector, Will and Aldo. They met twice a week at 8.30 for coffee and a bagel before playing tennis. The break-in had ignited their morning. Like the loss of the ficus trees, the theft would become part of their folklore, one of those running stories, easily accessed.

"Need any change for the float, Jack?"

They were men with time to be amiable. They liked

to laugh and had been around long enough to know that there are worse things in life than a till on the floor with its tongue out.

When Nessa came for lunch, Arlene was theatrically skirting around the two men from Ben's 2-Hour Glass ("If it's broke, we give you a break"). She held the plates high and stepped over their tool bags.

"If I fall, it's gonna cost Ben plenty."

One of the men was from Argentina – dark and good-looking with teeth from a Colgate ad.

"You fall, I catch you."

Arlene laughed and hoped he had not noticed the bruises on her left thigh. What on earth had made her wear shorts today? On the other hand, maybe the bruises would give him ideas. She realised she would like him to have ideas.

Jack had made two chicken salad sandwiches on rye and had sat down to lunch with Nessa.

"You look tired."

"It's not tiredness, Jack, it's cancer."

She picked up her sandwich and smiled at him.

"I slept ten hours last night."

He knew from her smile that his fussing had been forgiven. She was not always so lenient. She had dumped without explanation those friends who had displayed too openly their sympathy. "I can't be doing with the soft voices and dewy eyes," she had said. "It scares the shit out of me."

Jack understood her feelings but found it hard not to show his concern. Back in the '50s, his father had died of cancer. In those days cancer had been a voodoo disease. In his father's case, diagnosis to death had taken eleven months and not once in that time did Jack or his mother utter the dreaded "C" word. Indeed, the doctor had advised Jack's mother not to tell her husband that he had cancer. It was felt that it would not be good for his morale. Aged nineteen, Jack had been drawn unwillingly into the conspiracy.

Towards the end, when his father weighed less than seventy pounds and they had to give him the morphine by mouth because there was not enough flesh on his body for injections, his mother's concern for her husband's morale had struck Jack as ever so slightly irrelevant.

His father had died with his eyes open. Jack had been in the room with him – on the night watch, but asleep in an armchair. Something had woken him. He liked to think it had been filial instinct, but it was more likely the dawn light filtering through the cheap, unlined curtains. No matter, he had missed the final moment. Perhaps only by seconds, for the spittle on his father's chin was still glistening with air bubbles.

He had wiped it off with the edge of the sheet and closed his father's eyes. Only then did he call his mother.

"Thank God. He slipped away peacefully in his sleep."

"Yes," he had said. One more lie did not seem to matter.

Nessa's voice broke through his thoughts.

"I have to go – see you tomorrow."

"Sure, look after yourself. Is it O.K. to say that – not too concerned?"

"Bye, Jack."

Back at the house, Nessa put on a jacket and went out to the beach. She headed north, into a steady wind that slowed her pace. Usually she walked up to the Four Seasons before turning back, but today she had to settle for the Ritz Carlton, dropping down thankfully on to one of the sunbeds lined up on the sand. Strictly speaking, they were for hotel guests, but the beach boys knew her and looked the other way. She could measure her growing weakness by this daily exercise. She had gone from jogging to power-walking to walking – and now it seemed she was to become a stroller. How long before she was a shuffler? She closed her eyes and tried to think of happier times. As was happening more and more, she thought of Henry.

On the way to the airport, a crow had swooped low in front of the taxi and had been hit – the muffled thud like a door closing in a distant part of a house. Another day she might have thought it an omen, but not that day. She and Henry were on their way to New York for a delayed honeymoon – five whole days away from the office. They had stayed in a small hotel on 63rd Street between Madison and Park. The elevators had iron gates and the attendants were elderly men with white gloves. They always remembered your names: "Mr and Mrs Cage – eleventh floor. Goodnight, now." She said it was like being in a Frank Capra movie.

Nessa had promised to show Henry her home town but on their first full day it had been he who had set the agenda.

"How about lunch, a film and then dinner, but shopping first," he had suggested.

"I don't need anything," she had said.

"What's that got to do with shopping?"

They had walked up Madison Avenue looking in all the shop windows and by some happy chance, some unconscious harmony, not once in twenty blocks did they have to wait for the traffic lights at an intersection. On subsequent trips she saw how aware he was of the lights, varying his pace to avoid the short delay at the kerb, impatient, harried. For him "DON'T WALK" meant "START RUNNING". But on that day, the gods were with them. They criss-crossed the street – from bookshop to bookshop – over to the Frick, then back for the Whitney. The spring weather had beguiled the city. For once, New Yorkers were taking it easy, hustlers turned boulevardiers. As they passed the Carlyle, she knew that on this particular day, the tables would be full for afternoon tea.

She must have fallen asleep for when she opened her eyes the sun was low in the sky and the beach was in shade. It felt chilly. A small, yellow aeroplane flew by at the water's edge, trailing a banner advertising a bar in Delray Beach. She walked home, the wind now at her back. Inside the house, she went straight to the fridge. It was 6.00. In the bar at Delray Beach they would just be kicking off their Happy Hour. She poured vodka into a kitchen tumbler, pleased to know that she was not drinking alone.

13

Detective Sergeant Cummings had rung just before 8.00.

"Ah, glad to catch you before you go out. I presume, since we haven't heard from you, that things have settled down. No more trouble?"

Henry immediately thought of the three Polaroids tucked between the pages of *The Collected Poems of James Laughlin* – a volume he had judged unlikely to interest the browsing instincts of Mrs Abraham.

"No, nothing, I'm pleased to say." His hesitation had been imperceptible; or so he had thought.

"You're sure, are you, sir?"

"Why – do you think he'll come back?"

There was a long pause before the policeman answered. Down the line Henry could hear the scratch of a match.

"That's the second time you've made that assumption, Mr Cage. Well, let's say that you're right and it is a man – though I don't know what the evidence for that is, but let's say it is a man, then I wonder what's made him stop. You haven't paid him off, have you, sir?"

The question was asked with a chuckle and Henry took the cue and let it hang there, unanswered.

"You see, Mr Cage – this is what worries me; there's someone out there with a bee in their bonnet about you. They wish you harm, sir. One way or the other. I wouldn't want you not to take it seriously."

"I'll call you if anything happens." Henry recognised the routine insincerity of his response, "I promise, I really do."

It was too late. In mid-sentence, the detective had put down the phone.

Walking to the brasserie, Henry had felt uneasy about their conversation; not about its conclusion, but about its timing. Why had Cummings rung so early? And what was it that he had said? "Glad to catch you before you go out." It was as though he had known Henry's timetable, the precise moment that he left for breakfast. Henry pushed the thought away. He was being paranoid; the remark had no special significance; it was what anyone might have said at the beginning of a working day. He quickened his step, eager to see Maude.

A week had passed since their first encounter and he had begun to look forward to their conversations. She had still not told him why she had left Henry Cage & Partners, but yesterday she had said in reply to his repeated enquiry, "I'm not working this Sunday – buy me lunch and I'll tell you."

When he got to the brasserie, the non-smoking section was full. He had to sit among the puffers and coughers in the back room. He was irritated that Maude would not be serving him. He had hoped to talk to her about Sunday lunch. She had seen him and indicated that she would come over later. He ordered his usual decaffeinated black coffee and plain croissant (no butter, no jam) and opened his book.

On Sunday he dressed carefully, several times. He was increasingly disheartened by the images thrown back by the wardrobe mirror. In a sports jacket and tie he felt stuffy and saw himself sitting across from Maude like an uncle up from the country. In a suit, he was her bank manager. He took off his tie and opened the top button of his shirt. It was more casual, but when he lowered his chin a vertical fold of skin appeared. His head seemed to be perched on the neck of a turkey. Finally, he settled for a polo-necked sweater and a pair of cords. What did it matter? It wasn't exactly a date. Or was it?

He had arranged to meet her at the restaurant, a small Italian place where they knew him well. She had declined his offer to pick her up at her flat.

"Believe me, you don't want to see me on Sunday mornings until you have to. I'll be at the restaurant at 1.30."

Henry arrived early to make sure they had given him the table he wanted. It was at the rear of the room by two windows that overlooked a courtyard garden. He asked the waiter to change one of the place settings so that when Maude arrived they would both be looking into the room. He was never comfortable with his back to the action and avoided restaurants that could not offer him a round table and reasonable privacy. He opened his book. He was re-reading *A Game of Hide and Seek* by Elizabeth Taylor, a particularly English love story he had always thought and one of the best. He looked at his watch – good, he had fifteen minutes before she was due.

And that was how Maude saw him from the door. Head bowed, deep in his book. She noticed the long arch of his back, his shoulders frail without a jacket. It was the first time she had really looked at him.

"Hello, I see you've brought some insurance against a boring lunch."

He stood up and held her chair.

"It was only insurance against a boring wait."

When the menus came, Maude was decisive; gnocchi to start with, followed by lamb. She accepted with enthusiasm the offer of potatoes and spinach. Henry was amused. For years at business lunches he had sat opposite ladies who had ordered grilled vegetables with monkfish – and an espresso, thank you.

"You remind me of my ex-wife," he said.

"Is that good?"

"She loved gnocchi – all Italian food."

"Did she like it here?"

Henry realised that he had been tactless.

"No, this place wasn't here when we were together."

He was back in the lift again, metaphorically staring at his shoes, unable to think of anything else to say. He had steered the conversation into a cul-de-sac.

They were rescued by the arrival of a platter of *carta da musica* – crisp, paper-thin, sheets of unleavened bread, seasoned with rosemary and olive oil.

"This is special. The chef is Sardinian and . . . well, you'll see . . . it's completely addictive."

The awkwardness passed and over the next two hours they began the age-old journey from attraction to involvement. It is always a passage fuelled by confession. He talked of Nessa and the divorce, she of the man with the socks.

When it was time to go she invited him back to her flat. Inside the building she had kissed him – encouragement, she said, to climb the five floors to the attic. Once there, she led him by the hand into her bedroom. He was breathless from the stairs and hesitated at the door. She sat on the bed and lifted her shirt over her head. He gave an involuntary gasp. Her skin was olive and her breasts extraordinarily beautiful, unexpectedly full – the nipples ringed with bold circles the colour of milk chocolate. Later, he believed he had tasted vanilla in the creases of her body.

14

It felt good to be driving with her beside him.

For Henry, true intimacy in a car had always taken place in the *front* seats, not the back. He did not mean the head in lap kind of thing, though in his teens he had not been a complete stranger to that. No, the romance had been in the simple act of driving with a woman next to him. He enjoyed the obvious togetherness, the common destination and the pleasure in a shared landscape. He particularly liked driving at night, when the glow from the dashboard mimicked the lighting in 1940s black-and-white movies. At night, all his companions had been beautiful.

But best of all he liked the talk. He and Nessa had always had their truest conversations on long drives. In a car you are side by side, not looking directly at each other, warily watching for the minute tics and involuntary gestures that belie the spoken words. The Catholic Church, with its curtained confessional, had always known that face to face is no way to learn the truth. Analysts have us lying on a couch, none of that nonsense about looking each other in the eye.

He glanced at Maude's knees – less distracting now

that she had a road map resting on them. At Mildenhall, he had taken a wrong exit at the roundabout and she, realising his mistake, had found a left-turn that would get them back on course. In this manner they had discovered one of the most beautiful roads in England, the kind of road that immediately knocks 15 miles per hour off a driver's speed, for no traveller wants to leave it too quickly.

A lesson for our road planners, Henry had thought, composing in his mind a new letter to *The Times*. Perhaps trees and landscaping can achieve through beauty what speed guns and cameras have failed to do by threat.

The neatness of his argument was undermined by the niggling suspicion that speed cameras might have been effective. Never mind, he could re-work the argument to make the point that the advantage of beauty as a deterrent is that it causes pleasure not a resentment of the forces of law and order. Yes, there was something in that. He would think about it back in London.

He had slowed the car to 20 miles per hour and opened the sunroof. There was no traffic, most drivers preferring the sign-posted route to Brandon that takes them past the American Air Force base at Lakenheath, with its screaming jets and scruffy golf course.

This slower, alternate route undulates through the eastern edge of the Thetford Forest and seems like a throwback to the '50s, literally, a memory lane. Initially, the forest keeps its distance, recent felling opening up vistas on either side of the two-lane road. After a mile or so, the trees advance – first, strands of Scots pine and birch and then the full canopy of the forest itself arching over the road. Even in mid April, the architecture of the overhanging trees was thrilling and Maude had temporarily put aside her misgivings about the trip. At first, she had refused to come.

"Henry, it's an awful thing to do. You haven't seen Tom in years and then you turn up with some bimbo girlfriend."

"You're not a bimbo."

"That's what he'll think."

"It will be less awkward if someone else is there – less chance of recrimination. He can't be angry in front of strangers."

"You're wrong. It will be a disaster."

In Swaffham he pulled into the market square and rang Tom as requested – some culinary timekeeping demanded notice of his whereabouts. Henry had been mostly silent during the call and Maude had grown uneasy.

"Alright, I'll see you in about forty minutes." He put the phone down and turned to look at her.

"I need some air."

He did not move to open the door as she expected, but lowered his forehead on to the rim of the steering wheel.

"Henry, what's happened?"

He looked up.

"It seems I have a grandson."

She did not answer.

"They have a child. A boy. His name is Hal and he's

almost four years old, for pity's sake. Four years . . . and I didn't even know he existed."

He opened the glove box, looking for tissues.

Maude sat motionless in her seat, wanting to comfort him, but at the same time repelled by his distress. It made her feel uncomfortable. She noticed the softening line of his jaw, the tears on his cheek. What on earth was she doing here?

"I'm so sorry, Henry."

The road map was still on her lap.

"You can drop me off in Fakenham and I'll get myself back to London."

When he answered, she could hear the bruising in his voice.

"Would you? That would probably be for the best."

He left her at a hotel in the centre of town where she could get a taxi to Norwich and then the train to Liverpool Street. They had parted awkwardly.

"I must give you some money."

"I have a credit card."

"No, no."

He shifted on the seat, reaching into his trouser pocket. The seat belt made it difficult, but he did not think to release it. Maude sat looking straight ahead.

"I'm sorry it's turned out like this."

She took the money. He walked round the car and let her out. They did not touch. A flutter of hands and she was in the hotel.

It's over, he thought as he drove away. She's not going to sleep with a bloody grandfather.

Driving through a small town he saw a newsagent

with toys in the window. He stopped, hoping to find something for Hal. He tried in vain to remember what Tom had played with at four. A train set? Or was it Lego? In the event, it did not matter, for the main toy section on the first floor was closed. On Sundays, they sold only things for the beach – balls, kites, crab lines and fishing nets. He bought a kite that looked unlike any kite he had ever seen, assured by the teenage shop assistant that it would do the business.

He wanted to stop at a pub and steady himself with a large whisky, but feared arriving with alcohol on his breath. He did not want that to be his defining aroma when meeting Hal.

Outside Tom's village, he pulled off the road. He was shaking. He prayed that he would be able to hide his anger. He locked the car and, clutching the kite, walked into the village.

Tom and Hal were at the window of the front bedroom watching for the Mercedes.

"I guess it will be a Mercedes," Tom said. "That's what he always used to drive."

"I don't think he's got a car, Daddy."

At that moment Tom saw his father in the distance. He knew him instantly: the same spare frame, his hair still dark, and worn slightly too long as he remembered. As often with tall people, his father walked with his eyes downcast as though the ground were treacherous; but now the steps were more tentative and Tom realised that Henry was ageing and the knowledge made him gasp.

"There he is – that's him."

Hal was gone – out the front door and running

down the street, disregarding every parental warning. From the window Tom saw that the road was safe and fought back the inclination to shout out a warning. He saw the small boy run up to the man and stop. He saw the man kneel down and place a hand on the boy's shoulder, the kite lowered carefully to the ground. They were talking, the boy uncharacteristically still as one question followed another. When the man finally stood up, the boy held out his hand and brought him to the house.

15

"Grandpa, do you like organic vegetables?"

The boy had insisted that Henry should sit next to him at lunch and had kept up a merry chatter throughout the meal.

"They're very good for you, you know."

Henry had told a story. Once on holiday with Nessa in Venice, they had sat next to a large party of American socialites at lunch. The hostess was a woman called Nan something or other – he had seen her photograph in magazines. The women were all thin and more vivid than their menfolk. They were on their sixth carafe of wine and the talk was careless. They were discussing wealth and an Englishman had said in all seriousness, or so it had seemed to Henry, that "the main difference between the rich and the poor is that the rich eat smaller vegetables".

Tom and Jane had laughed, but Hal had been puzzled.

"Excuse me, Grandpa, we eat small vegetables, but we're not rich, are we, Daddy?"

After lunch they had taken the kite to the beach at Salthouse. The wind had been perfect and the kite had performed as promised. There had been a tacit agreement to fill the afternoon with activity. When the wind dropped, Hal took charge, recruiting his grandfather to search for the white round pebbles he needed for his collection. On the way back, they had made a detour to show Henry the duck pond by the roadside.

"Watch the cars," Tom had said.

Several of them were parked at the water's edge and at intervals a window would be lowered and a handful of bread thrown on to the water. Sated swans ate only the food that fell into their immediate orbit, content to let the ducks and gulls squabble over the rest.

They went back to the house for tea.

"Why don't you and Hal go up and make the toast, while I give Henry a tour of the shop."

If it had been pre-arranged, Jane had made the suggestion seem entirely spontaneous.

There were three rooms given over to books, each with a couple of chairs for reading. In one room there was British fiction, in another, American novels and short stories, and in the third room, poetry. The shelves were full and there were vases of spring flowers on the window ledges. He hoped there would be time to browse after tea.

"He's been so excited and nervous about you coming."

"He is a wonderful little boy."

"Yes, he is wonderful – but not so little. I'm talking about Tom."

Jane opened the door to the office.

"Come and sit down, Henry, I want to show you something."

The office had a window overlooking the salt marshes. Henry perched himself on the edge of a chair looking out on to the view. Jane had gone back into the shop.

"You're probably familiar with this."

She had brought back a small, blue, cloth-covered book. He looked at the title: *Journal of Katherine Mansfield.*

"Yes, I know it."

"When we started the shop, some of the stock was ours – books we owned – and some we got from book fairs and house sales; rather a mixed lot."

She was talking slowly, as if reluctant to make her point.

"Sorting them out, I flicked through this one, the way you do – and I noticed an underlining; the only one in the whole book. I thought the person who did it must have been so unhappy."

She gave him the book, open at the right place. He would always remember that the lines were at the top of page six:

> It is as though God opened his hand and let you dance on it a little, and then shut it up so tight – so tight that you could not even cry.

The underlining, in pencil, was not a neat and studious exercise aided by a ruler, but two, deep, freehand wounds in the paper. Henry was suddenly fearful.

"And then I turned to the front and saw Tom's signature; it was one of his university books."

She was standing in front of him, her arms crossed over her chest, holding herself so firmly that her fingers had almost disappeared into the folds of her woollen sleeves.

"Living all these years without you has been tough for Tom. If you ever reject him again, I promise you, I will haunt your days."

She let her hands fall to her side.

"Come on, let's join the men."

Following her up the stairs, Henry thought, My God, how Nessa must love this woman!

After tea and toast, Hal had climbed on to Henry's lap and clasped his face, the little fingers warm on Henry's cheeks. Then with the gentlest of pressure, like a good barber, he had indicated how he wanted Henry to move his head. He had studied Henry's face in silence, as though committing it to memory. Then with a smile he had hopped down from the chair.

Henry had left half an hour later. He had asked after Nessa, but Tom had said that she wanted to give him all the news herself. They had walked back to the car with him. Strangers driving through the village would have seen a family tableau – a pretty woman with corn-coloured hair, linking arms with an older man, the other two, so obviously father and son, skipping on ahead. "Ahh," they might have exclaimed.

Back in London, Henry checked his messages. There was nothing. He realised that he was disappointed. He had a shower but knew he would not sleep. His head was too full of the day's events. It had been a good day;

better than he could have hoped for, the day he became a grandfather, the day he had been re-united with his son and Jane. So why, he wondered, was there no elation?

He went downstairs and made a coffee, careful to choose the decaffeinated beans. In the drawing room, the shutters were open and there was enough light for him to see what he was doing. The Polaroids were still there, entombed in their book of verse. He looked again at the splayed legs of the head-butter's girlfriend, thinking of Maude.

16

He had always had a temper. A short fuse, his mother had called it – said it twice to the magistrate. She had been wearing a black wool suit from As Good As New, a genteel, second-hand shop just off Elyston Street. It was July and nearly ninety degrees and most of the people there were in cotton and linen. He was ashamed of her red face and damp hair. He knew she had bought the suit to impress the court. As if the magistrate would not know, just by looking at her, that tomorrow she would be mooching around in a cotton shift with bra-straps slipping down her fat, mottled arms. Colin did not dislike his mother; he just couldn't stand the sight of her. Even as a young boy he had rejected her taste. He would not wear the T-shirts she bought with their Disney tack and patterns and would hold out for solid colours. He had grown up sleek and stark and full of scorn.

In court that day, she had spoken of her son's violence as though it were dandruff, unattractive but passing. The magistrates had weighed her care-worn loyalty against the boy's record and sentenced him to nine months at a youth correction centre near Croydon.

He had spent his sixteenth birthday there. Joe the

warden and his wife had laid out a few bowls of crisps and a birthday cake on the table-tennis table. He remembered the cake; a shop-bought Victoria sponge with sixteen previously owned candles ringed around the edge. Some of the candles were so stunted, it was unlikely that the flames would last long enough for Colin to draw breath. He did not even try. Before Joe could light the blackened wicks, Colin had fled to his room.

Within a week he had started cutting his arms. He had managed to hide it from them for a couple of months, but one day in the washroom, Joe had come in unexpectedly and seen the fine tracery of scars on Colin's arms. There had been a few sessions with the regional psychiatrist and they had decided to send him home three months early. The cutting had stopped as soon as he was back in London. His mother had wanted him to add to his three O-levels, but all he wanted was work and money. He was tall and strong for his age and had been taken on as "the boy" by a scaffolding company. The work was good – it paid well and he liked being up high, looking down on people. He lived with his mother in her council flat off Ebury Street, casually slapping her whenever the mood took him.

He heard the bleep of a monitor; they must be checking his blood pressure. He was conscious that his left arm was raised high, in some kind of a sling. He looked up and saw that he was on a drip as well. He was surprised. All this for a broken arm? Come summer, he would have to go through airport security with two steel plates in his arm. Can't put them in a plastic tray, can you? Not that he had any cash for a holiday – he would not be back on the scaffolding for a while, if ever. Not much call for a bloke with a weak arm. Shouldn't have lost it with Big Dave; not a floor up, that's for certain.

He frowned at the memory of his fall and the scuffle that had preceded it. A brawl later denied by both men to a succession of cynical listeners: the boss, the union official, a bored policeman.

There was the click of high heels in the corridor. He relaxed. That will be Eileen, maybe she will have some good news. As the drugs claimed him once more he comforted himself: he had seen the way men looked at her body, there was money in that sort of look. Drifting off, he wondered what the old perv with the Mercedes had thought of the photos.

The next day he was up early.

"Your girlfriend looks nice." Marlene, the Irish nurse, was getting him ready to go down for his X-rays.

"She's nice enough."

"Oh, I can see you're a sweet talker."

They showed him the X-rays. He had snapped both the bones in his left forearm. Now the breaks were straddled by two steel plates, the screws clearly visible. The surgeon was pleased. They had been clean breaks. He did not anticipate any problems. When the swelling subsided they would put on the plaster cast, which he would need to wear for six weeks.

Back in the ward, he asked for more painkillers and slept. When he awoke, the afternoon had gone and

Eileen was sitting by his bed. She had brought grapes.

"Very original."

"They're seedless. I thought they're easier to eat."

"I've still got one hand – and I can still spit."

"Sorry."

Careful, keep it down, keep it down; what did the shrink at the remand home say? Count to ten and think of something pleasant. Jesus, seven years' training to come up with that. Don't upset the girl, though. Go easy.

"I'm sorry. It's the pain."

Look at her, eyes brimming over.

"Come back tomorrow, I'll be better then. Sorry, and all that."

He closed his eyes and heard the rustle of paper as she put the grapes on the locker. Did she say goodbye? Next day, he could not remember.

17

Mrs Abraham had her routines. On Mondays, she did the washing and ironing. She liked to come in about a quarter to nine, get the machines going, and then sit at the kitchen table with her *Daily Mail* and a coffee until a beep from the laundry room told her that the first wash was ready. She looked forward to this leisurely prelude to the working week. Monday was the only day that she did not read her newspaper on the bus. She had built a life of carefully contrived small treats and she understood the value of postponed pleasure.

When she saw Henry at the kitchen table, still in his dressing gown – a cup of steaming coffee at his right hand and *The Times* laid out before him, she had not bothered to disguise her irritation.

"What are you doing here?"

"Good morning, Mrs Abraham."

Henry had been tempted to mention that it was *his* house and that he even had the right to breakfast at his own table, but caution prevailed. He sensed that his unexpected presence had ruined Mrs Abraham's morning. A man of fixed routines himself, he was respectful of the agendas of others. Besides, she was very good at ironing his shirts, savvy enough to know that one ironed *away* from the collar points. Such expertise was not to be jeopardised in this day and age.

"It's just a one-off. Sorry. Business as usual tomorrow."

The following morning he arrived at the brasserie five minutes before it opened. Peering in, he could see waiters standing in the shadows. He tried to identify Maude, but the figures were indistinct, only their white aprons detectable in the gloom. He had a premonition that she had left, that he would never see her again. He knew that he could find his way to her flat again, but he would not try. If she had moved on, it was a clear sign that she did not want to see him and he would not go where he was not wanted.

"Is Maude in today?"

He had tried to make the question seem casual, planning his movements in advance. He saw himself as in a movie, a cup of coffee held halfway to his lips – a smiling, urbane man pausing to ask the kind of polite question you would ask – no more than a regular customer enquiring after a familiar waiter, small talk as you settled the bill.

"She doesn't work here any more. She phoned in yesterday."

"Oh." He felt his stomach lurch, but took a sip of coffee to show that the news was inconsequential, "I hope she's gone on to something exciting."

"I doubt it."

He left a tip, larger than usual. On the way out, he saw the head-butter's girlfriend sitting alone at a window table. He looked away, but not before their eyes had met. He was not sure, but he thought she had smiled at him.

Out on the street, a crowd was emerging from the underground. People with fast walks and destinations. He was caught in their flow until the traffic lights at Lower Sloane Street halted the tide and he was able to peel away into the square. He walked to the fountain. The pond had been drained for the winter, but there had been enough rain to coat the bottom with a soupy mix of leaves, fag ends, paper bags and God knows what else.

As he watched, a police car bullied its way round the square, its siren screaming. The morning stretched out in front of him. He decided to walk around until the bookshops opened. There, at least, he would find diversion, if not solace.

Crossing the King's Road at the junction with Cadogan Gardens he heard the sound of men shouting. A small crowd had gathered and he joined them. A van driver, young and large, was exchanging obscenities with a taxi driver, small and old. Both men were out of their vehicles, squaring up in the middle of the road – traffic building up behind them, horns blaring.

"You don't park on zigzags, you cunt – you fucking idiot."

"Why don't you just piss off?"

As Henry watched, the slanging suddenly turned to wrestling, the bigger man holding the cab driver in a head lock, and all the while screaming at him "You don't park on zigzags, you fucking arsehole." He was jerking the smaller man up and down and the taxi driver, short of breath, had stopped answering back.

Henry looked at the people around him. Most of the men were smiling and quite a few of the women, too. Just imagine the hilarity if the big chap managed to break the little man's neck! What a laugh that would be! Henry pushed through the crowd.

It had been surprisingly easy to part the two men. He had simply walked up to them and said, "Calm down, or you'll get yourselves into trouble."

The van driver had backed off and Henry had shepherded the older man back into his taxi.

"I wasn't parked on the bloody zigzag, I was letting someone off."

The fire had gone from his belly and he was no longer the tiger of five minutes ago. He sounded worn and querulous. Henry closed the taxi's door.

"Just go. It's not worth it."

The fun over, the gawpers and the grinners had gone on their way, but Henry had stood there, elated. There is always pleasure in taking responsibility when others shirk it, and the incident had reminded Henry of his days at the company. He had felt in charge. Sheer vanity, of course, but he was reassured to know that he could still act decisively when needed.

Cheered by this knowledge, he abandoned his trip to the bookshop and made for home. On the way, he made his second decisive move of the day. He stopped at a travel agency and bought a ticket to Miami, for a flight leaving in three days' time. He had decided to bring forward his trip to Florida. He would forget Maude by remembering Nessa.

18

The Ritz Carlton in Palm Beach is proud of the paintings on its walls. Guests are encouraged to take a conducted tour of the rooms and corridors, though in fact, most of the good paintings (if you like liberally varnished nineteenth-century landscapes) are to be found just off the lobby in the ground-floor lounge and bar.

It is here that people take afternoon tea and meet for pre-dinner drinks. In the evening there is a piano player and if you are back late from a concert it is a good place to snack on spring rolls, *filet mignon* or a sandwich. You will always find somewhere to sit – that is, from Monday to Friday.

At the weekends, it is standing room only. The hotel books a dance band, four musicians and a singer – old hands, who are rarely stumped by a request. Most of the people who fill the plump chairs and sofas at the dance floor's edge are not guests, but local residents. The few tourists lured on to the floor by the familiar strains of Gershwin and Porter are easily identified by their lack of finery. The locals make an effort, the men in slacks and jackets, the women dressed for a party in chiffon and satin. The results are plucky rather than impressive. Designer gowns from a former era, lovingly preserved in polythene, hang uneasily on bodies that have had no such luck. Some of the couples have obviously danced in competitions in the past and for them the dance floor remains an arena. In the confined space they somehow manage to impose themselves, gamely re-running their ballroom triumphs.

Jack and Nessa are younger than the other dancers and not part of the clique. They sit at the back of the room, distanced from the musicians so that they can hear themselves talk when not dancing. Lately, they have been doing a lot more not dancing. When they started coming two years ago they would be up for every jig. Now, on a good night Nessa might manage one in four.

"It's not all bad, Jack," she says as they sit down, "it gives us more time for drinking."

A waitress had followed them to the table with a bottle of red wine. She was a student who worked part-time and Jack knew her. In the long summer vacation she had sometimes helped out at the café.

"Hi, Kara, how's it going?"

He noticed the damp stains on the girl's ankle-length skirt.

"Been better, I guess?"

The girl frowned as she wrestled with the corkscrew. The cork refused to leave the bottle.

"I can't believe this is happening to me. I can feel myself blushing."

"There's no rush, we're not going anywhere."

Twenty-five miles away, Henry was also not going anywhere. The cab taking him to the hotel from Miami airport was gridlocked on Interstate 95.

"How far to go?"

"Oh, we're about halfway, sir. Traffic will ease up once we're past the Fort Lauderdale intersections. You take it easy now."

Henry closed his eyes. It was 1.00 in the morning, London time, and he was tired. When they finally arrived at the hotel he had been asleep for an hour.

"We're here, sir."

Dimly, he heard a second voice. A man in a uniform was opening the door.

"Welcome to the Ritz Carlton, sir."

The warm night air invaded the car's interior, surprising him. Under the hotel's covered portico, cars were waiting to be parked. The owners, fearful of losing their slots in the Grill, had abandoned their vehicles, leaving doors open and headlights blazing as they grabbed their tickets. Over the hum of the idling motors, Henry could hear music – the tempo of a foxtrot curiously choreographing the darting runs of the valets as they parked one car and hurried back for the next. He paid the driver and then, bleary-eyed, followed a bellboy into reception.

At the desk there was a line and he wandered into the lounge. White heads bobbed on the dance floor and he turned away. A few minutes later he was escorted to a suite on the ground floor. He was told that he had direct access to the ocean but was too weary to pull back the curtains. He would check it out in the morning. As Henry fell into a dreamless sleep, Jack and Nessa, somewhat unsteadily, got to their feet for the last waltz.

Henry was awake at 5.30. He put on a dressing gown

and went out on to the terrace. The air was moist and a stiff breeze from the south ruffled the palm trees on the narrow lawn that separated him from the beach. In the blackness, he could hear the clamour of the ocean. His room faced due east and he sat on the terrace waiting for the dawn, drifting in and out of sleep. At 8.00, he was woken by bright sunlight shining in his eyes. He showered and changed into shorts and a T-shirt and went looking for breakfast. The restaurant was almost empty and he was shown to a table by the window. Below him he could see the swimming pool. He thought he would spend the morning there before seeking out Nessa.

At the buffet he picked up a bowl of blueberries and a croissant. Carrying the plates back he saw that a couple with four young children had sat down at the table next to him. The father was in his mid-thirties, lean with a boyish face and sandy hair. His wife, it seemed, had dressed in a hurry. Her sneakers were unlaced and not all of her T-shirt was tucked into her shorts. Her hair was still damp from the shower and she and the children sat slumped in their chairs as the father, too loud and cheery for the hour, took control.

"What's the agenda today? The pool? That's what I'm saying!"

Henry took another look outside. The pool area seemed large enough to avoid Daddy's bonhomie.

Half an hour later, Henry had positioned himself on a sunbed by the deep end of the pool. He imagined that the young children would be confined to the shallow waters at the other end. The family arrived soon after and settled themselves alongside Henry. It quickly became obvious that the four children were already contenders for the U.S. swimming team. One of the boys was particularly adept at swimming underwater. He would push off, arms to his side, and glide almost the length of the pool before surfacing. Each time he did this, his father would burst into song.

"They call him Flipper! Flipper! The king of the O-C-E-A-N!"

Hearing the chorus for the tenth time, Henry left for the beach.

He decided to walk south into the wind, reckoning that he might need help from the breeze on the way back. It was Sunday, but at this hour the beach was almost empty. Two joggers passed him, cheerful women with enough stamina to shout their greetings.

In the distance he could see a figure standing at the water's edge. He found the walking hard going, his feet slipping in the soft sand. He went closer to the water looking for a firmer footing. He had not realised how unfit he was. To get his breath back, he stopped and feigned an interest in the dark bulk of a container ship inching along the horizon. After his walk, he would see if the hotel had a gym. He turned south again, now walking on a gritty strand of the beach that gave him more purchase, but hurt the soles of his feet. The figure in the distance was now walking slowly towards him. He could see that it was a woman. He pondered in advance the etiquette of passing a lone woman on the beach: was it correct to say "Good morning," or should one avoid eye contact and walk by silently as though deep in thought? The problem was solved for him.

"Henry? I can't believe it. Is that you?"

In a movie they would have run towards each other as the violins soared, but here in real life, Henry had to fight an impulse to turn and hurry away. The voice was unmistakably Nessa's, but even from fifty yards he could see that this woman was not Nessa. She continued walking towards him, her knees too prominent, her thighs thin and wasted. Beneath her floppy sun-hat he could see nothing but the glint of dark glasses. Oh God! Please let it not be Nessa! He had stepped off the strand of shale and his feet were sinking into the sand. He stopped walking and waited for her.

"Henry, why didn't you tell me you were coming?"

She clung to him and kissed him on the cheek. He turned for the second kiss, but she had reverted to the American custom and stepped away. Embracing her, he had felt her hip-bone, its hard edge like a diagnosis.

"I wanted to surprise you," he said.

"Well, you succeeded."

She had removed her sunglasses and he could see her face.

"I'm sorry. I never knew."

"I didn't want you to know. What could you do?"

That night they went to dinner in Palm Beach. The restaurant, booked by Henry through the concierge, was slick and commercial. The risotto they ordered appeared almost instantly. It was sticky and straight from the microwave. Obviously, there had been no chef in the kitchen with twenty-five minutes to spare – no purist prepared to add the broth to the simmering rice slowly, spoonful by spoonful. They were offered dessert within forty-five minutes and were out the door within the hour. At the kerb, a valet ran forward to collect the ticket for their car.

"I hope you had time to park it."

"Yes, ma'am," the young man said, Nessa's sarcasm wasted.

Back in the king-size bed in the ducal suite, jet lag and grief combined to keep Henry awake. He had his radio with him but in America even the 2.00 a.m. talk shows are too vibrant to dull the senses. The nuts are nuttier, the angry ones angrier and he turned the dial hunting boredom. For a while he thought he had found it on a religious channel. The preacher was sonorous and simplistic. Henry closed his eyes and prepared for sleep, but the preacher man was just getting into his stride.

"God," he intoned, "is like the good pharmacist, measuring out our medicine, so that we get not one particle more than is good for us. NOT ONE PARTICLE MORE! He never sends us more pain than we can handle."

"What goes wrong with suicides, then? You smug bastard!" Henry shouted out loud.

19

Aged thirty, Maude had so far avoided serious disappointment – not because her life had been blessed, but because, until now, she had been careful. If she saw unhappiness on the horizon she ducked down a side street and took a different route. At university she had gained a reputation as a tease. She was flirtatious and enjoyed the intellectual challenge of courtship, but rarely would she take the relationships further. She liked novels where lovers are separated by fate or duty, but remain true to each other. She would joke (only half-joke) that unrequited love is the only kind of love that lasts.

Sleeping with Henry had been an act of kindness. She had been nervous about shagging a man only a few years younger than her father – not an ageist thing, she had told herself, more a matter of aesthetics. As Henry had undressed she saw with relief that his body was not repulsive. His legs were free of the knotted veins she remembered well from her father's rare ventures on to the beach.

Henry had come to her bedroom like a visitor to a museum, expecting to look, but hesitant to touch. Their love-making had been friendly and conversational. Not fireworks, but good enough, he hoped. He had found her body beautiful and had told her so. When he got up, she had remained in the bed, watching him put his clothes on, knowing that he would find it disconcerting. She had turned on the bedside television while he was still on the stairs.

At the time, she had thought they would go on to enjoy a sentimental friendship, punctuated every so often by sex, but not about sex. She understood that Henry's agenda might be different; for she appreciated his need for physical reassurance, but she had never doubted that he would settle for her terms. What choice did he have? When she thought of their future together, they were never in bed, but in Paris or Rome – walking by day, then dining at night beneath the trees, the heavy silverware catching the last gleams of a setting sun. She laughed at herself, but the adolescent images persisted. She had even planned the routes of the walks they would take, the hotels they would stay in. She imagined unhurried time with him.

Seeing him distraught on the trip to Norfolk had unnerved her. It was not merely the new complications in his life that had disturbed her, but the way he had looked in anguish. For the first time she had seen him in an unfavourable light and it had been "*finis*". It was a shallowness in herself that she acknowledged. In the past she had ended comfortable relationships because a man, good in every other way, had turned up for a date in trousers too low on the hips or had tipped his head too far back when drinking. Brown eyes, smoking, jewellery, heavy watches, facial hair, bad teeth, an over-large knot in a tie or an undersized gratuity at a restaurant – for Maude there had always been countless hurdles on the road to love. Now, it seemed, she had added a soft jaw-line to the list.

The journey back from Norfolk had been tedious. The taxi driver had been content to sit behind the swaying rump of a caravan all the way to Norwich. It had taken her more than four hours to get to London.

The following day she had phoned the brasserie and told them that her mother was ill and she had to go back to Bristol. She knew that Henry would come looking for her with apologies and tales of his grandson and she did not want to be around when he did. She had to be gone before the daydreams returned; the bijou breakfast room at the Hotel Montalembert with its warm baguettes and ramekins of Normandy butter – and then the stroll to the Jardin du Luxembourg to see the small boys with their pond boats, all of it as charming as ever.

20

Nessa had decided to email Tom and Jane.

The cancer had not impaired her handwriting, which still retained its youthful vigour, though mysteriously these days her spelling had become unpredictable.

She would know when a word looked wrong, but she could not always call up the right combination of letters to put it right. If she did not nail the word first time she was stuck, for she hated to use a dictionary. She was like one of those male drivers who would rather stay lost than stop the car and ask for directions. Last month, she had bought herself a computer that corrected her spelling for her. She now sent emails with capital letters, punctuation and conventional spelling. She hated the abbreviated texts she sometimes received in return.

"Since there's no restriction on space," she would reply, "why turn a message into a puzzle? Please, send it again in English."

My dearest Tom and Jane,

Do you know that Henry is here? It's so good to see him! I couldn't believe it. There I was, out for my early-morning stumble on the beach when I saw this man at the water's edge looking out to sea. It's true what they say in the novels – I went weak at the knees (not so difficult in my case) – at that distance he was only a shape, but I knew it was him. I can't run nowadays, but my heart was racing instead.

I could tell he wasn't sure it was me. I had my floppy hat on and dark glasses and as you know my body is, well, different. I think he wanted to run away, but I called out – and then we met and held each other. (Briefly, but it was the first time in years.) The joggers were kind enough to run around us.

Poor Henry, everything's hit him at once. Did you think he has changed? I do. He's less certain about things – not surprisingly. I showed him some photographs of Hal as a baby and he broke up. I know he was dreadful after the divorce, not answering your letters, but I wish we hadn't kept Hal from him. It was cruel, don't you think so now?

We go for quiet meals together and talk. I could say a lot more, but it's probably enough to say that I'm happy. What would make me even happier is if you could bring your trip forward and come out and join us. Would Miss Martha let Hal miss a few days of school? He's so young. It wouldn't harm, would it? Let me know if it's possible.

All my love, Nessa xxx

P.S. Tonight, Henry is meeting Jack for the first time. I do so want them to be friends.

After Ocean Avenue crosses the Intracoastal Waterway it continues for about a mile before it reaches the intersection with U.S.1. The road remains flat, but the neighbourhood goes downhill. The store signs are suddenly brash, anticipating the competition of the Highway ahead. The local Hair & Nail, a modest business with four chairs and a permanent staff of two, optimistically announces itself with a two-storey sign on top of its one-storey building. Opposite, a fibreglass marlin leaps through the roof of a fishing-tackle shack. Close to the road, the deli has rigged up enough neon to constitute a driving hazard.

Only two enterprises hold back; a florist's where the grimy windows disguise the fact that what's on offer is an Interflora service and not flowers, at least, not real ones. By the door, half a dozen silk blooms gather dust in a dry bucket. Like plain pets in a dog's home they have been waiting a long time for someone to take them home.

Next door to the florist, forming a little enclave of non-aggression, is an Italian restaurant. It is a family business that for thirty years has been content to let its food do its advertising. Nessa has booked a corner table for 8.00.

"Henry, why don't you sit yourself in the middle, looking out. Jack and I have been here so often we *know* there's nothing to see."

The restaurant is catching its breath after the bustle of the early-bird crowd and not all the tables are taken.

"The hectic time here is between 5.30 and 7.00 p.m. The old-timers eat earlier every year. Soon the doctors will be advising anyone over sixty to get all their eating done before noon," Jack explains.

Henry looks around the room. It's true – apart from an elderly couple dining with a middle-aged woman presumably their daughter, the oldies have gone home and the crowd is quite young. The place feels intimate, the lighting soft, the once-white tablecloths laundered to a low-wattage grey. A tropical fish tank acts as a room divider, screening the diners from the reception area by the front door. Henry tells the story of a client who installed a £40,000 aquarium in his corporate lair. It took up the whole of one wall facing the client's desk. The office joke was that the fish found it relaxing watching the boss work.

The story reminds Jack of Terry Cartwright, the owner of a recording studio in New York. He, too, had fish tanks around the place.

"Terry was a big guy, must have been 300 pounds easy – a fabulous eater, who lunched at the same place downtown every day. He had this nickname, 'Terry Two Cabs'. Everyone called him that, not to his face, mind you. The story goes that his secretary had once sent a cab to pick him up from the restaurant at the usual time of half after two. At three, the restaurant had rang her asking if she could send another cab. They said Terry had eaten the first one."

Henry learned that Jack had been an actor in New York.

"My career wasn't distinguished, but it was consistent. When I wasn't waiting table, I was waiting around."

Henry had smiled.

"And then I lucked into doing some voice-overs –

that's how I met Terry. I was good at it. I could do accents and read fast. Pretty soon, I stopped going to auditions and just did radio commercials and voice-overs for television ads. It was well paid, but essentially a foolish business. If you've got any brains you can only do it for so long. Maybe that's why I lasted twenty years."

Henry had always thought it strange that America, such a bold and swaggering presence on the world stage, liked its humour to be self-deprecating. Over the years he had run into countless Americans who had belittled themselves to raise a smile. It was often disarming, though he had soon discovered that it was not always a guarantee of humility.

"I know a little about it," Henry said. "I feel sorry for the people who do it. It seems to me they usually get thirty seconds of time to accommodate fifty seconds of script."

"Yes, that, and more. I've got some out-takes of a session Orson Welles did for Findus Foods. I'll play it to you sometime. Orson hated doing it. Me, I just took the money. Lots of it. When I came down here, I didn't need to work. I planned to be a tennis bum, but I got bored, so I bought a place where I could wait table again. How crazy is that?"

Nessa relaxes. She has eaten very little, but if the men notice they say nothing. The talk has been light, the subtext of the evening ignored. As Jack and Nessa confer about a dessert wine, Henry sees a slight commotion at the table of the elderly parents and daughter. The father is getting up, the women holding out restraining rather than helpful hands. The man persists, though he has trouble straightening his legs once he has hooked them from under the table. Once upright, however, he has no trouble walking. He is wearing a pale-green corduroy suit, unique in this room of short-sleeve shirts and chinos. It gives him an academic air, an impression that is heightened when he speaks. He has stopped at the table next to Henry's where two couples have been enjoying a boisterous evening as three bottles of red wine have followed two rounds of pre-dinner cocktails.

"Would you mind keeping the noise down, please. We're finding it difficult to hear ourselves think."

On his way back to his wife and daughter, the man smiles at Henry as though Henry has been complicit in the complaint. There is a lull. The offending diners are stunned into silence, but only momentarily. One of the women says loudly, "Well at least we're not all half dead."

"Speak for yourself," Nessa says.

21

"I've got something to show you."

Eileen fished in her bag and brought out an envelope from Boots.

"I haven't had a chance to look at them myself yet."

Colin watched her carefully lift the flap of the envelope and take out the wallet of photographs.

He was sitting there fully dressed. As soon as the doctor came round and gave the O.K., he would be free to go. He had been in hospital for five days, longer than anyone expected. He had reacted badly to the anaesthetic. Blood pressure too low, or something. His arm was now in plaster from below his elbow to his fingertips. The blokes in the ward had wanted to scrawl a few greetings on his cast, but he had told them to forget it. If he had to wear the bloody thing, the plainer the better.

Eileen showed him the photographs, holding them up like the "show-and-tell" cards her mum had used with her little brother when he was behind with his reading.

"Next."

They were all of him.

"Next."

She must have taken the pictures the first night he

was in hospital – while he was lying there, drugged up and well out of it. Given that the prints were from Boots, the quality was not bad.

"Just keep them coming, will you?"

She had used the angle-poise on the bedside table as a light source and the screen around the bed to bounce the light back on to his face. Quite arty-farty. For one close-up she must have had the camera down by his chin, pointing up. His swollen black eye looked like a blue hill, the stitches on his eyebrow showed up as stunted trees against the skyline. She was a quick learner. The swelling had gone down a bit since then and the stitches were coming out in two days.

She was looking pleased with herself. "Not a pretty boy, then?"

"Yeah, you didn't have to take a whole roll to prove that."

"Well, what do you think?"

"I think you should stay your side of the camera, that's what I think."

He could tell she had used his Leica. It was the first camera he had ever owned; stolen it from the glove box of an Alfa when he was twelve. Normally he would have passed it on, but there was something about the way the camera felt in his hands, and he had decided to keep it. For weeks he went around with the unloaded camera clicking at this and that. The shutter action was so quiet it was like a spy camera. It went on from there; even when the thieving and temper landed him in various correction centres, he went on snapping. Now he had three cameras – the Leica, a Nikon and a Polaroid for the bedroom. He vowed he would never go digital.

He had met Eileen when he was doing an evening a week at the local camera club. Glamour shots. Most of the tossers who turned up were pathetic – just there to poke their lenses into places they had no hope of poking their dicks. For him it was about money. Eileen had been booked as a model. She wanted to be the next Sam Fox, but she was better than that. Not as big, but better.

They had a drink after the session and he had offered to give her some help. In a month, she had moved in and they had been putting a portfolio together ever since. She was a natural, not one dodgy part on her body. Usually there was something to hide; if they had a great backside the face would make you throw up. Very few had a full deck. She would not let him do porn on a proper camera. It was fine on the Polaroid for them, but not for the book. He could wait. For the time being there would be money enough in the Page Three shots. Anyhow, the Polaroids had come in handy to wind up that freak in Chelsea. He had got that right. When he had looked in the window he had seen the paintings on the wall. The man obviously liked naked.

22

Whenever Henry was away, Mrs Abraham found time to do a few little extras. Henry was a tidy man, but inevitably he left his mark on the house. There were splashes on bathroom mirrors, smudges on doors and cupboards from hands blackened by newsprint. In the kitchen she found smears of shoe polish on the floor and in the hall there were always kick-marks on the skirting board under the mirror. Mrs Abraham noted the signs of Henry's occupancy with a cold eye and cleaned up behind him. By the time she left the house at 1.00, only the clothes in the wardrobes would say that this was a house where a man lived alone.

When he travelled she did the things she could not manage in a normal week: shampooing the carpet, washing the paintwork, getting the curtains to the cleaners, or most fiddly of all, dusting the books. That Henry never noticed these ministrations did not discourage her. The enemy was dirt. It was her own private war.

With the books, she did a shelf at a time, starting with the top shelf and working down. It was obvious that Henry did not arrange his books logically or by category. Nevertheless, she imagined that he had a system and it was not for her to question why a gardening book by a Russell Page should be next to a memoir of a life in the theatre by a Peter Brook. She took great pains to ensure that each and every book went back to its pre-allotted space. In point of fact, Henry did have a system, based on the height of the book and the colour of the book jacket's spine. He avoided colour clashes and blocks of a particular colour and tried to space taller books at intervals across a shelf so there was a uniform look. If the spine proved too vibrant to fit in, he would simply throw away its dust jacket. He was slightly ashamed of this system and knew that the disposal of the jackets was financial folly.

Mrs Abraham was at the top of the stepladder when the Polaroids slipped out of the book. As fate would have it, like toast, all three photographs fell butter-side down. She came down the ladder still clutching the host volume of poetry and expected she would be retrieving some misplaced pictures of a young Tom or of a smiling Nessa.

She turned over the two close-ups first – so the final picture came as something of a relief. She realised that she had thought the close-ups were of Nessa. It was not that Mrs Abraham was particularly shocked. Sex was sex and bodies were bodies and she had done enough laundry in this house to know that it had never been a convent. But for all that, she did not have Nessa down as someone who would open her legs for a camera; at least, not with a straight face, so to speak. So who was this girl? Did Henry know her?

She had sometimes wondered what Mr Cage had

been doing for sex since the divorce. Whatever it was, he had not been doing it at home. For a year or two, she had come in on a Monday morning alert for a whiff of perfume in the air, for evidence in the bed or bathroom, but there had been nothing. No contraceptives in the cabinet, no sweet messages on the answering machine, no letters of endearment in the toast rack. She was beginning to doubt that he was actually alive down there.

She took the photographs and the book to the chair by the window and sat down. This needed thinking through. Her first instinct was to put the photographs back in the book, no-one any the wiser. But what if Henry had kept the photographs at a particular page in the book? She fanned the pages to check that there were no others tucked in somewhere and noticed handwriting on the title page. She knew at a glance that it was not Henry's.

"*First U.S. Edition. £40.*"

Of course! The book was second-hand! That was the answer. Mr Cage had probably shoved it straight up on to the shelf, unread. He could not possibly read all the books he ordered. He had only been away a week and already there was a stack of catalogues waiting for him on the kitchen table. Content now, she took the Polaroids into the kitchen and put them in the bin. On Thursday they would be in a landfill. No need to torment him with what he could not have.

She returned to her work and dusted her way down the shelves. She was thorough and had a respect for books. If it was a gardening book or something on architecture she would occasionally pause to look at some of the pictures. It took her two hours to do the books in the front room. She decided she would tackle the library tomorrow.

At ten past one she left. She was running a little later than usual, but there was no rush, her afternoon job did not start until 2.00. She locked the three locks on the front door, the top one so high she had to stand on tiptoes.

When she turned round a young couple were standing by the gate admiring the garden. The woman was taking photographs.

"Does look nice, doesn't it? You should see it in the summer." No need to mention that the garden did not belong to her.

"Not long to wait, then."

The young man seemed affable and opened the gate for her, slightly awkwardly for one of his arms was in plaster.

"We always stop and look at this garden."

"Yes, it's lovely."

The woman had lowered the camera. A pleasant voice and Mrs Abraham smiled. It took her a moment to realise that she had seen this woman before. But this was the first time with clothes on.

"Oh, I'll forget my head one of these days. I've left my purse inside." She hurried back along the path.

In the kitchen, she retrieved the photographs from the dustbin and got the steps out again to put them back in the book. If they were in the wrong place, so what? Mr Cage would be too embarrassed to mention it.

23

That evening, Jack had arranged a poker game with his tennis pals and had cried off the dancing at the Ritz Carlton. The previous week they had gone as a threesome. On that occasion, apart from two visits to the bathroom, Henry had sat in his chair, social enough, but not dancing. There had been a period in the '60s when the easy rhythms of the twist had got him on to the floor, but when Chubby Checker had checked out, so had Henry.

Now, without Jack, he was not sure of his role.

"Don't worry, Henry, we don't have to dance. Though, it wouldn't harm you to walk me round, just once. Nobody will be looking at your feet. Indeed, I rather hope that everyone will be looking at *me*."

Nessa sat on the edge of her chair. She had done something to her hair. It was pulled back so that her face, no longer framed by a dark bob, appeared less pallid. She was wearing green silk, the colour of moss kept short of daylight. The gown was high on the neck, long in the sleeve, and when she walked the full skirt caressed the ground. She had bought the dress the day before on Worth Avenue and the effort had sent her early to her bed. But the dress was a triumph. Hidden in its silken folds she felt whole again, even glamorous. She gazed at the dancers, longing for Henry to take her arm.

He watched her and misread the brightness of her eyes. She had always looked tenderly on public displays of affection and he knew that the couples on the floor would delight her. Henry saw only elderly people dancing, but she would see enduring love, the survival of romance. He knew he had the power to make her happy. He knew she wanted a public confirmation of their togetherness, partners in more than a dance. All he had to do was hold her hand and walk forty steps on to the dance floor and then take another hundred while he was there. What was the big deal about that? Why did he hesitate? He saw her knee lift and fall under the silk of her gown, her tapping foot betraying her eagerness to dance. Even now, at the fifty-fifth minute of the eleventh hour, he held back. Why? It was cruel and stupid. When this dance was over, he would ask her for the next.

"I got cleaned out, so I came over. My God, Nessa – you look wonderful, that is some frock!"

Jack did not sit down but hovered, waiting for the music to stop. When it did, he offered Nessa his hand.

As she stood, she looked at Henry.

"I'll get some more wine," he said as they walked off.

24

Jack drives a 1962 Impala station wagon, sprung like a bed and as wide as a dinghy. At a pinch the two bench seats can take eight people and there's still an acre of space for stuff in the back. He had bought the car when he first came down to Florida. He had chosen it not for its utility, but as a symbol. Confirmation that he no longer wanted a slot in the fast lane. The B.M.W.s he had once owned he now derided. "I'm out of the race," he said. As the years went by, it became clear to his friends that he had not left the race; he had redefined it.

Now he drove doggedly in the centre lane, no more a speedster, but a self-appointed arbiter of vehicular character. Anything post-1970 had little chance of earning his approval. He reserved his most withering scorn for people-carriers.

"You get a lot of seats and no luggage space, or a lot of space and no seats. Some deal! This beauty gave you both – still does."

They were driving to Miami airport to pick up Tom, Jane and Hal and one hour into the trip Henry had realised there was no need to reply.

On cue, a Chrysler carrier drew up alongside in the

outside lane, its headlights flashing at a slow-moving Ford in front.

"See what I mean? It's just a van in Sunday clothes. Slap a sign on the side and it could be full of dry cleaning or copper tubing. Whatever happened to style?"

As the slab-sided Chrysler cut into the middle lane, Jack was glad of the opportunity to press the chrome bar on the steering wheel and send out a reproachful bleat.

"I love that sound," he said. He pushed the bar again, unconcerned that the mellow note fell on deaf ears. The Chrysler had already lurched back into the fast lane and was moving on.

"You want to hear that Orson Welles tape?"

"Fine."

"You know the set-up? Orson is in the sound booth and the film is on a loop coming over on a monitor so he can sync. the words. He can see the sound engineer through the window and they can talk to each other over the intercom. There are a couple of agency guys in there with the engineer – usually the copywriter and a producer – and they kind of direct the thing."

Jack pushes the button and Henry feels a rush of pleasure as the rich tones of Citizen Kane and Harry Lime reach to the furthest corners of the Impala.

ORSON WELLES: "We know a remote farm in Lincolnshire where Mrs Buckley lives. Every July, peas grow there" – do you really mean that?

AGENCY PRODUCER: Yeah, so in other words, I – I'd start half a second later . . .

ORSON WELLES: Don't you think you really want to

say "July" over the snow? Isn't that the fun of it?

AGENCY PRODUCER: It's – if, if you could make it when that shot disappears it would make . . .

ORSON WELLES: I think it's so nice that you see a snow-covered field and say "every July peas grow there". "We know a remote farm in Lincolnshire where Mrs Buckley lives – every July, peas grow there" – we aren't even in the fields, you see. We're talking about them growing – and she's picked them.

AGENCY PRODUCER: In July . . .

ORSON WELLES: What? – I don't understand you then – when? What must be over before "July"?

AGENCY PRODUCER: When we get out of that snowy field.

ORSON WELLES: Well, I was out. We were on to a can of peas – a big dish of peas when I said "in July" . . .

AGENCY PRODUCER: Oh, I'm sorry.

ORSON WELLES: Yes, always. I'm always past that.

AGENCY PRODUCER: Yeah?

ORSON WELLES: Yes! That's about where I say "in July."

AGENCY PRODUCER: Will you emphasise "in". "IN July".

ORSON WELLES: Why? That doesn't make any sense. Sorry, there's no known way of saying an English sentence in which you begin a sentence with in and emphasise it. Get me a jury and show me how you say "IN July" and I'll go down on you. It's just idiotic – if you'll forgive me for saying so. It's just stupid. "IN July" – I'd love to know how you emphasise "in" in "in July". Impossible! Meaningless!

AGENCY WRITER (in an attempt to placate): I think all they were thinking about was that they didn't want . . .

ORSON WELLES: He isn't thinking.

AGENCY WRITER: Orson, can we have just one last try? It was my fault. I said "in July" – if you could leave "every July"?

ORSON WELLES: You didn't say it! He said it, your friend. "Every July?" No, you don't really mean "every July" – that's bad copy. It's "in July". There's too much directing around here!

Henry was saddened by the anguish in Orson Welles' voice. The agency people were obviously English and maybe Welles had been careful to huckster only outside America, but it appeared the distance had not been great enough to spare him embarrassment. Why did he do it? Was there a roof to repair on a weekend house or a divorce settlement to fund? Maybe he told himself that he was in good company. Sir Laurence Olivier had touted Kodak film on American television and even Mrs Roosevelt had made commercials for margarine. Probably, Welles just wanted the money. Politicians and actors are precarious earners so the urge to cash in while the going is good is often irresistible. In Henry's time, a former British Chancellor of the Exchequer had genially promoted smoked salmon for a supermarket. He hated to see them do it. Even when he had been commissioned by a client to find a spokesperson he had been secretly pleased when he had been met with a refusal.

Jack forwarded the tape, chuckling in anticipation. "Just listen to how the session ends."

The dark brown voice once again filled the car:

ORSON WELLES: Here under protest is "Beef Burgers". "We know a little place in the American far west, where Charlie Briggs chops up the finest prairie-fed beef and tastes . . ." This is a lot of shit – you know that? You want one more? More on beef?

AGENCY PRODUCER: You missed the first "beef" actually. Completely.

ORSON WELLES: What do you mean missed it?

AGENCY PRODUCER: You're emphasising "prairie-fed".

ORSON WELLES: But you can't emphasise "beef" – that's like wanting me to emphasise "in" before "July". Come on, fellows, you're losing your heads. I wouldn't direct any living actor like this in Shakespeare, the way you do this. It's impossible!

AGENCY PRODUCER: Orson, you did six last year and by far and away the best – and I know the reason . . .

ORSON WELLES: The right reading for this is the one I'm giving you.

AGENCY PRODUCER: At the moment.

ORSON WELLES: I spend twenty more times for you people than any other commercial I've ever made. You're such pests! Now what is it you want? In the depths of your ignorance, what is it you want? Whatever it is; I can't give, deliver, because I just don't see it.

AGENCY PRODUCER: That's absolutely fine . . . it really is.

ORSON WELLES: No money is worth this . . .

His voice tails off. There is a heightened rustle of paper as he picks up his scripts from near the microphone, and then all is silence. It is the kind of silence you get in a cinema at the end of a powerful movie when the audience is reluctant to re-enter the world outside and sits motionless through the credits, right through to the Dolby logo.

Jack turns off the tape.

"What do you think?"

"It's very sad."

Jack was unrepentant.

"He took the dough; no-one said it was an easy job. Anyhow, it still makes me laugh – and he did walk out – I never had the guts."

They drove in silence for a while.

"What time do they get in?"

"Same time as the last time you asked me. The plane gets in at 3.30. And the flight's on time."

Henry looked out of his window. The Interstate was frantic with Sunday traffic. Drivers less concerned than Jack with the aesthetics of motoring were passing the Impala on both sides. Henry was thinking of the previous evening.

After her dance with Jack, Nessa had seemed radiant on returning to the table.

"Did you see me, Henry?"

"Oh, yes."

She had reached for her glass, but put it down without drinking. Then, sitting back in her chair, she had closed her eyes. They thought she was listening to the music, but it soon became clear she had fallen asleep. Ten minutes later she awoke and had asked Jack to take her home. She had said goodnight to Henry without looking at him.

"I called Nessa this morning. She's got her machine on."

"I know," Jack said.

"Do you think she's O.K.?"

"It was a new dress, Henry. And she didn't buy it for me."

The reproach was not unexpected, but its curtness irritated. There was a kind of laconic, Will Rogers sagacity about Jack, as though in his youth he had watched too many westerns where the heroes had spat out more tobacco juice than words. Henry suddenly yearned for the unstudied remark, the incoherence of careless anger.

"No, she didn't. So what were you doing there? Just do me a favour and shut the fuck up."

"*Carpe diem*, Henry. Seize the dame."

Henry slipped low into his seat and put his feet up on the dashboard, cheerfully aware that Jack would be worried about the paintwork.

They drove without talking, both men surprised by Henry's outburst.

Tom and Jane had travelled light, their soft duffel bags an easy fit in the overhead lockers. Living on the beach presented few sartorial challenges and what summer clothes they needed they kept permanently at Nessa's house. On this trip they had brought nothing but shirts and shorts for a growing Hal and gifts for Nessa. A few days before, she had emailed them asking for two Ordnance Survey maps of Norfolk – sheets 132 and 133.

"I'll be able to pick out your house and remember our walks along the coastline," she had written. The email's implicit acknowledgement that his mother would never visit Norfolk again had alarmed Tom. Now just two hours away from seeing her he felt nervous. He tightened his grip on the trolley as Hal pulled them eagerly into the arrivals lounge.

"What are those men doing?"

"They're drivers, Hal. On the cards are the names of the people they've come to collect."

"Someone's collecting me then."

It was Hal who had seen the two men first. They were standing amongst the waiting drivers and Henry was holding a sign: the boy's name written in red capital letters on the back of one of Jack's menus.

25

Maude had retreated to her mother's side looking for comfort. What she had forgotten was that her mother had never been remotely comforting. Mrs Singer was a quiet woman who lived in a quiet house with a largely silent man. She was a tax accountant with a local firm, where her lack of exuberance had soon propelled her to a senior position. Her husband was an insurance broker and commuted to High Holborn. On weekdays, they both dressed in similarly conservative suiting. She wore the collar of her white shirt folded outside the lapels of her jacket in the manner of cricket stars of the 1950s. He buttoned his shirt at the neck and set it off with one of his five weekday ties, worn in strict rotation, each one as reticent as the next.

Since the birth of their daughter in 1969, Mr Singer had adopted the role of junior partner in the marriage. He had an exaggerated regard for the bond between mothers and daughters and when Maude had become serious about a career in ballet he had been overjoyed. This indeed was woman's work, no need for him to get involved.

It was Mrs Singer who had juggled her work hours to ferry Maude to and from her lessons in Bristol. It was

Mrs Singer who had driven her to London for the interviews at the Royal Ballet School and she who signed the cheques that had kept her there.

Confronted by a wilful child, Mrs Singer had been dutiful, nothing more. She had seen that Maude was already, at fifteen, the wrong shape to be a star: too long in the body and too short in the leg to aspire for anything better than the back row in the corps de ballet, and someone else's corps de ballet at that, not – definitely not – the Royal Ballet's.

So it had proved. Maude had moved from one small company to another, dancing in minor European cities, often on stages erected in piazzas and parks. The music was always recorded, no orchestra within twenty kilometres of the performance. When Maude had tripped over a speaker cable and injured her knee, it had provided her (and all concerned) with an honourable exit.

Mrs Singer had remained supportive, but unconvinced, when her daughter had turned to History of Art. Why, she wondered, could her daughter's generation not just get a job? Why all this need for fulfilment? Was a career that put food on the table not good enough? Why did it have to feed the soul as well? Never having looked for such bounty herself, she was bemused by her daughter's expectations.

Maude had long recognised the muted nature of her mother's support. At the Ballet School's end-of-year performance, invariably staged at a real theatre, and sometimes at the Opera House itself, it was mandatory for the parents, relatives and friends to give the cast a standing ovation.

As the dancers took their final bows, Maude would see her mother drawn to her feet by the example of her neighbours – applauding, yes, but the only parent in the auditorium who managed to do it without smiling.

Emotion was avoided in the Singer household. Never once had Maude heard her parents raise their voices. From the age of twelve, the silence at family meals, companionable to her parents, had been torture for her. The clink of the cutlery, the moist smack of their chewing and their audible swallows had driven her, more or less permanently, from the family table. She had contrived to be at friends' houses at mealtimes, or, failing that, would invent hosts and eat at the Telcote Café, near the school. She funded her meals by judicious dips into her mother's purse, noticed by Mrs Singer but ignored. When seen occasionally by staff, eating her supper at the Telcote, she would explain that both her parents had jobs that kept them working late. At parent-teacher evenings, the Singers were greeted with the cold courtesy reserved for inadequate parents.

Maude stayed in Bristol for three days. Her decision to go back to London had been greeted with neither obvious relief nor entreaties to stay longer.

"I'm off," Maude announced.

"I expect you'll sort things out, Maude. You usually do."

This pleasantry was delivered as Mrs Singer sat on the half-landing loo, her voice just loud enough to penetrate the door.

Maude had been halfway down the stairs on her way to the station.

"Thanks for the tête-à-tête, Mum," she had called out.

A week later, Maude returned to work at the brasserie. She was behind with her rent and needed money more than she needed escape from Henry. The time away had eased her anxiety about seeing him again. He was, after all, a sensible man and she could deal with his hurt feelings. It had been a mistake getting that close, but no real harm had been done. She reminded herself that she had always been good at closing things down and the foolish dreams of Paris and Rome had disappeared. But despite her best intentions, she found herself looking for Henry each morning and the slow realisation that he had changed his routine had irked her. It was a blow to her pride, if not her heart.

The weather had become warm, a southerly wind bringing a false spring to London. The tables on the pavement had suddenly become popular and she was glad of the extra activity. Being busy meant more tips and less time for thought. She was aware that she was in a state of limbo, in a meaningless job with no attachment to anything or anyone. On her days off she stayed in bed. Until her first pay day there was little food in the flat. At the staff table, she ate as heartily as was seemly.

One night she returned late from work and found a letter from Henry on the ledge in the ground-floor hallway. She saw with a sense of puzzlement the American stamps. On the back of the envelope he had written "If not known, return to sender" and his London address. She had climbed the stairs and fallen on to her bed before opening the letter. It had been written on hotel notepaper.

Dearest Maude,

I don't know if this will reach you. They told me at the brasserie that you had gone home to Bristol. I'm hoping that you have arranged for your mail to be sent on. As you can see, I'm in Florida and will probably be here for a while. I'm writing to apologise for being so mawkish in the car that day.

Love, Henry

She folded the letter carefully before tearing it into small pieces.

26

When he hit Eileen he was always careful to open his hand and just give her a slapping around. He could not afford to leave any bruises that the camera would pick up. Especially not now when she had just got her body all over a brochure for a local tanning parlour. Not the kind of job he really wanted for her, but it was a start.

"Sorry, love, didn't mean to lose it."

"Yeah, well you didn't lose it enough to put a mark on me, did you?"

She would sulk now for a few days. It used to be that he could talk her round in no time.

"I'm sorry."

"Piss off. You don't care about me. You going to be around when I'm forty and my tits are on the floor? I don't think so."

"That's a long way off, love." Colin forced a smile and put his arm around her bare shoulders. She shrugged him off.

He slapped her again across the ear. She shrieked and fell on to the bed, her knees pulled up against her chest.

"I'm going out."

At the door he looked back at her and went down

on one knee. It was a nice shot – if you had the camera here the punters could see everything.

When she heard the outside door close she went to the window. They were living in his mother's council flat although his mother was not there. She had found her son's contempt more bruising than his fists and had unofficially moved in with her sister in Ealing.

From the window Eileen saw Colin cross Ebury Street, walking fast. She knew he was going to the gym. He was keen to build up the muscles in his injured arm. He had told her he was going back on the scaffolds as soon as he was fit; he said he missed the lads.

Her head was hurting and she was tempted to lie there and fall asleep, but she had to be at work by 9.30. She had run up a lot of jobs since coming to London, mostly in shops. She would stick them for a while and then get fed up with working on Saturdays and go on the dole. At the moment she was working in the Body Shop, which Colin in a good mood had said was appropriate. She quite liked it there. It smelt nice and was close to the flat and there were no men on the staff. Men meant gropes in the stockroom and jokes about her chest.

In the bath, soothed by sustainable tree oils from somewhere in South America (she couldn't remember where) she weighed for the umpteenth time the pros and cons of leaving Colin. On the plus side, she still fancied him. He was not bad in bed, but she was never sure he enjoyed it. Often, it was bang, bang and all over, like he had needed a glass of water. But there had been worse, and he was clever and knew about photography.

He had got her the tanning parlour job – £200 for two hours' work – and even though he had kept half for himself, it was her first bit of modelling and the start of better things to come. She believed him about that. On the down side, she knew there was something freaky about him, like stalking that bloke in Chelsea, dragging her round to take pictures of his house. What was that all about? Sometimes he frightened her. Not just the hitting, but the moody stuff and silences. Often, he would not talk to her. He could spend thirty minutes polishing his shoes and not say a word.

She suspected that he didn't really care about her. He was just using her; but then in a way, she was using him, too.

Drying herself in front of the mirrored wall, she dropped the towel and stood waiting for the glass to demist. When she could see herself, she struck a pose, copied from the Marilyn Monroe poster she had in her bedroom at home – hands clasped behind the head, weight on the left leg, right knee slightly bent, belly pushed out – yes, she looked good. She let her hair fall forward, screening her face.

27

"Why don't you guys go some place on your own?" Jack was looking at Tom and Jane.

They were all outside, sitting on the deck. Jack had come round for supper. Henry was going to barbecue later.

"What a great idea," Nessa said. "Tom and Jane, please go – you've not had much time to yourselves, have you?"

"Yeah, and take my car, not that tinny rental thing you've got. Go in style, my friends."

So it was decided.

Tom and Jane left in the Impala, bound for Boynton Beach and a place that Jack had recommended, right on the waterfront.

"Order Rum Runners and conch fritters and you won't go far wrong," he had said. "And no second rum for whoever's doing the driving."

He was only kidding about the second drink, he said, but they all knew he wasn't.

The food was good and by the time they had finished eating, the waiters had lit the candles on the tables.

"It's beautiful here. It feels wrong to be happy – but here, right now, with you, I am."

Her eyes were full of tears.

"I brought her a cup of coffee yesterday and I was almost on her before she saw me."

"I know; but she's peaceful, don't you think? Tying up all the loose ends, righting all the wrongs. Dad is here – it's all she wanted."

"It's too late – why didn't he forgive her years ago?"

"It was just so public – if it hadn't been in the newspapers, he wouldn't have minded so much."

"Yes, but."

"I guess if you spend your life shaping other people's reputations, it's easy to end up caring too much about your own."

Tom had shrugged; the little-boy shrug that had been passed down from Henry to Tom and that was now hard-wired into Hal. No D.N.A. confirmation needed for these three, Jane thought – the lineage is there for all to see. Hal is a diminutive Henry in more than name.

"I do like your father, you know," she said.

"I know you do."

"Did you hear him reading to Hal last night? He must have gone through *Little Red Train to the Rescue* at least six times."

Tom laughed.

"Hal told me. He said Henry does all the sound effects. It appears his engine puffs are better than mine."

In the parking lot, they stopped in the shadows and kissed. She pulled him close.

"Promise me we'll never be like Nessa and Henry," she said.

When they got to the Impala, it would not start. Tom went back into the restaurant and rang Jack at the house.

"Stay by the car and don't let anyone touch anything. I'll come in your rental and you can drive it back. I'll be there in fifteen minutes. Don't try the ignition again. Don't drain the battery. Do nothing. It can't be anything serious."

"How was he?" Jane asked on Tom's return.

"He thinks we've destroyed his car."

28

Henry walked with his head lowered, watching his feet move across the sand. He was pleased to see that they still fell pointing straight ahead. A young woman bustled past him. As she moved away he noticed that despite a trim figure she was condemned by the splaying of her feet to walk the walk of the overweight. Her left foot landed at ten to the hour and her right at ten past. Such is the randomness of grace, he thought.

It was 8.00 in the morning. Calm weather – the sea as flat as a blue patch on a paint-chart.

Henry looked at Nessa. "No sign of Hal?" Their grandson was a boy who woke and left his bed in one single motion and he would usually accompany them on their early-morning stroll.

"If he wakes, he'll know where to find us."

"You're weaker than yesterday?"

"Yes, a bad night."

She adjusted her step. The ocean had coughed up a jellyfish on the sand.

"Do you remember when you refused to have me back and I went to Tom and Jane in Norwich? Do you know where I went after that?"

"Here, I thought."

Her breathing quickened and the grip on his arm tightened.

"I'm tired, let's sit for a while."

He led her to the low wall that fronted the next house on this stretch of the beach. It was as far as she ever walked now – no more than two hundred yards each way. They sat with their backs against the rendered concrete. Even at this hour the wall had stored heat from the sun and Nessa was reminded of the kitchen garden at Holkham in Norfolk where espaliered apple trees basked on red brick walls. She had liked the way they had spread their limbs to receive the sun and now she stretched her own arms in homage.

He waited for her to resume the conversation. She had closed her eyes and he searched for her hand.

"No, I didn't come back here right away. I rented a cottage up on the coast at Wells-next-the-Sea. I was there for a month. The cottage was not normally rented out, so it was full of stuff. Lots of paintings and books. In the living room the mantelpiece was crammed with old toys; cast-iron piggy banks, a sailor, a hen and a monkey. And I remember there were toy cars from the '30s and the wooden spoons and eggs for races. And, oh yes, there was a wooden pig that walked down an incline; but the thing that became important to me was a sort of Victorian building set. It was made up of little wooden tablets that had fingers on each end that interlocked. The tablets had letters on them and the owner had built a pyramid that read from the top down.

W
ILL
NOT
FALL
APART

She spelt out the letters for him.

"Later, I found a box in a cupboard and that was the name of the set – WILL NOT FALL APART."

Henry looked at her. "And you didn't?"

"It became my mantra. When I was alone on the beach and howling with grief, I would repeat it: will not fall apart . . . will not fall apart . . . will not fall apart . . . They were the worst days of my life and no, I didn't fall apart. So I won't now. That is, if you'll help me?"

"Of course."

The talking had tired her. She needed to gather her strength for this final request. Just before Christmas she had been experiencing double vision and a scan had confirmed that the cancer had spread to her brain. They had put her on a course of radiation and chemotherapy and for a few weeks her sight had improved, but last night she had told Henry that her vision was once more deteriorating. She was finding it difficult to move her left eye.

"I want you to go back to England. I don't want Hal to see me when this all happens. He's too young – and besides, he shouldn't miss any more school."

"I don't have a school to go to."

She shifted her weight and rested her head on his shoulder.

"Henry Cage, I love you so much I could die. But that doesn't mean, my darling, that I want you here to watch. It could take weeks, months – who knows? Come back to say goodbye. Jack will call if I can't."

In three days they were gone. In their luggage, Nessa had hidden letters to each of the adults and there was one for Hal, to be given to him when Tom and Jane thought fit.

A week later, wearing a jaunty black eye-patch, she took up residence in the palliative care unit of a hospital in West Palm Beach. She brought with her one small suitcase and arrived in an old Impala station wagon.

Mrs Abraham folded her newspaper.

"I'm sorry. I'll get back to the laundry. I'm just upset, that's all."

Yesterday morning, she had been surprised to see him in the house. He had not slept on the overnight flight and wanted to get to bed, but had waited to talk to her before going upstairs. He had explained the situation and she had listened in silence.

"It is what she wanted, Mrs Abraham. To go into the hospice and for us to come back for a while. Oh, and she gave me this letter for you."

He handed over the sealed blue envelope, addressed to "Peggy".

Mrs Abraham had put it into her handbag. She would read it later at home, she said – not on the bus; it was bound to make her sad and it would not do to let go in public.

The next morning, she had busied herself in the

laundry room until her coffee break. Then she went upstairs and read Henry the letter.

Dear Peggy,

I have missed you and the house and the garden so much. Thank you for helping me over the years and for being my friend. We did have fun, didn't we? Take care of Henry for me, he's such an old muddle and he'll probably be impossible for a while. I'm not in pain and feel calm.

Much love, Nessa

"How could you, Mr Cage, not be out there with her? I don't care what she said. You can take it from me she didn't mean it. Only thinking of you, she was."

The possibility that Mrs Abraham might be right did not occur to Henry.

Nessa had always been a straight-talker. If she had wanted him to stay she would have said so.

"It's what Nessa wanted, Mrs Abraham. That's all I can tell you."

"But didn't *you* want to stay, Mr Cage? Didn't you want to be with her for every single minute she had left?"

"I wanted what she wanted."

She looked bewildered, shaking her head, before going downstairs.

29

Sometimes when privacy was required Ed Needy would meet interviewees outside the office. This was normally the case when the company was trying to lure a star from a rival firm. These high-flyers were nervous about meeting on the premises and usually suggested a drink after work or, increasingly nowadays, breakfast. Which is why Ed was sitting at a table in the Sloane Square brasserie waiting to meet a young woman who was terminally disenchanted with her current employer and, most recently, her New Year bonus.

A chat with Ed was the last act of the hiring drama. He handled the discussions about salaries, expenses, cars and occasionally even stock options – what footballers and their agents now call personal terms. He was good at it. His first aim was to secure the services of the person in question, but if he could save a couple of thousand on his given budget – and he usually did – he knew it would be noted on the top floor. He had recently been promoted Head of Human Resources for the U.K. and Europe and his ambitions did not stop there. Still only thirty-five, he thought himself well positioned to be running the whole company one day.

After all, in an industry where the inventory goes

down in the lift each night, who better than a "people person" to run things? That he knew the nature of the skeletons in the management cupboards he also counted an asset. He was a patient man and had kept his ambition well hidden.

Henry had been one of the few who distrusted him.

"There's something creepy about him, don't you think? That silly way he holds himself when he talks; always fifteen degrees off the perpendicular. He doesn't even look straight."

He was chatting with Charles before a board meeting where Ed Needy had been asked to present the costs of a staff audit. The audit had been Henry's idea.

"Why don't we find out what the staff really thinks of us? We'll get an outside research company to interview everyone not on the board – anonymity guaranteed – and then we'll present the findings at a staff meeting. I'm sure we'll learn a great deal, good and bad."

Ed had been given the task of putting some numbers to the proposal. He had briefed a research company whose fee would be £30,000. The interviews would take a month and the report a further fortnight. At the meeting Henry had argued that they should go ahead, but had discovered that he was in a minority.

Roy had been emphatically against.

"It is far too much money and it will just stir things up. It will be a lightning rod for all the discontent in the company."

"If there is discontent in the company, don't you think we should know about it?" Henry enquired mildly.

"Of course, we should, of course." Charles leaned

back in his chair. "But there are other ways of finding out. We're all pretty good at reading the company temperature – you, Henry, best of all – and my own opinion is that there's not much wrong with morale that a few chats with department heads would not winkle out. And £30,000 plus, is a lot to pay for letting off a little steam. I suspect the staff would rather have it added to their next Christmas bonus. What do you think, Ed?"

Henry had waited for Needy to make his usual anodyne reply. His standard technique was to re-state the options with all their advantages and drawbacks, but never to take a position himself. But this time he had surprised Henry.

"I'm inclined to agree with you, Charles. Personally, I don't think morale's much of a problem at the moment. Sure, there are growing pains and perhaps a little stock-taking is a good idea, but I think we should keep it in-house. I suggest we talk to the department heads, as you said, Charles, and then I could conduct, say, twenty-five random interviews myself. We'd end up in the same place having saved ourselves thirty grand on the trip."

"And do you think the staff would talk openly to you? Do you think they would believe your promise of anonymity? Do you think we'd get at the truth if you did the interviewing?"

"Yes, I do."

In answering Henry's question, Ed had looked not at him, but at Charles.

Henry realised there been some pre-meeting collusion; Ed had been too pat with the details of his in-house scheme, but at the time he had failed to recognise the full significance of Ed's new independence. Two weeks later, Henry had been ousted and everything was clear. Ed would have been part of the prior discussions of Henry's compensation package. At the board meeting, he had known that Henry was no longer a player – he had become a man of no account.

Now, six months later, the new Head of Human Resources was growing impatient. The bloody woman was late, not a good omen, but Roy had been adamant that this one must not get away.

Rosemary Middleton had made her name in North America helping a former monopoly telco hang on to more than its fair share of a newly democratised market. The tactic had been to offer the public a raft of special offers and new tariffs and then rely on confusion and inertia. Faced with a complex choice, the majority of people had done nothing. The new telephone companies, despite their lower prices, were for the most part spurned. The free marketeers who had championed the breaking of the monopoly could do nothing. In an open market, it is not illegal to bewitch the public.

Rosemary, according to Roy, had written the book on the subject.

His mobile rang.

"Ed? I'm so sorry. Some thoughtless bugger decided to jump in front of a train at South Ken and nothing's moving. I'll go back up and grab a cab. Should be with you in ten minutes."

He beckoned a waitress, damned if he was going to wait.

"What would you like, Mr Needy?"

And that was how – after a formal interview and another lunch at the Connaught, Maude Singer had ended up working once more for Henry Cage & Partners; this time as personal assistant to the new Head of Human Resources for the U.K. and Europe.

She no longer ridiculed Ed's habit of tilting his head in conversation; she had, on the contrary, persuaded herself that it was rather endearing.

30

Dear Jack,

I'm not surprised that Nessa is the star of the show. She always was. In London, we would be walking down the street together and I'd suddenly realise that she was no longer with me. I'd look round and she'd be forty yards behind me, talking to a shop-keeper or a neighbour, or a stranger who had stopped to ask the way. If Nessa didn't know the directions, she'd rope in the next passer-by and pretty soon she'd have a small crowd around her, all trying to help.

In our patch you couldn't walk more than a few yards before someone would be waving to her – and not just from across the road but from cars and bi-cycles. She knew all the street cleaners, the dog walkers, the dustmen, the postmen and the gardeners – even the builders working in other people's houses. When new residents moved in they were told by the estate agents to talk to Nessa about help in the house, window cleaners and the local shops. She was the fixed star in our street's universe. And it wasn't just because she worked from home; it was because she was Nessa. I know that now.

You probably heard that I spoke to her on the phone last night – not for long, because she was tired. She told me that her eyesight has all but gone. I don't think I can wait it out here, Jack – I feel so distant. I'm at Tom and Jane's for the weekend, so I'll see your next email up there. When I'm back in London, I'll book a flight to Miami. Thanks for being there.

Henry.

It had been Hal who had invited Henry to Norfolk. He had rung early one morning.

"Grandpa, can you come and see us?"

There had been some whispered prompting in the background.

"This weekend, I mean."

"Oh, hang on a second, I'll see if I can find Grandpa – this is Albert Entwhistle here. I've just popped round to fix Grandpa's shower. Who shall I say is on the phone?"

"It's Hal." Henry heard the uncertainty in the little voice.

"Right, I'll give him a shout."

Holding the phone away from his mouth and continuing with the Lancashire accent, he raised his voice.

"Henry, there's someone on the phone called Hal. He wants to talk to you."

He held the receiver close again.

"He's just coming."

He heard Hal telling his parents what was happening. "I think it's Grandpa, just pretending."

"Hello, Hal, is that you?" This time he spoke in his normal voice.

"It was you all the time, wasn't it, Grandpa?"

"No, it was Albert Entwhistle."

The boy laughed.

"Will you come and stay with us this weekend?"

"I'd love to."

"And Grandpa – don't bring Albert."

In Florida, on one of their early-morning walks, Nessa had suggested that he should buy a weekend place in Norfolk.

"I'm not sure that Tom is ready for that."

"You're wrong. We've talked about it. They would both love you to be up there. You'd see a lot more of Hal."

"Nessa, you're a conniving old woman."

"It's a good job I am."

It had been agreed that Tom and Jane would look out for a property for him. Nessa suggested that it should be an edge-of-village house so that Henry would have no trouble finding a cleaner. She thought the house should be, at least, a twenty-minute drive away from Tom and Jane. (You can be too close to your relatives, she had said.) Oh, and no ponds or rivers in the garden – far too dangerous for children.

"Please do this for me, Henry. I love seeing you with Hal; it reminds me of how you were with Tom when he was little."

"I hope I'm better than that."

He drove up on the Friday evening to find that they had arranged for him to look at a house the next morning. It was called White Horse Farm and he was relieved to discover that the name was misleading. The house sat in only three acres of south-facing garden, the fields and woodland sold off years ago. Two brick and flint barns flanked what had once been the yard; it was now grassed over and planted formally with three rows of hazelnut trees.

At supper they looked at the estate agent's brochure, Hal turning to the floor plan and pointing to the bedroom he wanted when he came for a sleepover. They were booked in to see the house between 9.30 and 10.15. Twenty people were scheduled to look at the house over the weekend and twelve had already seen it. According to the agent, several of them were considering putting in offers. North Norfolk was fashionable and property prices were already at a level where they were causing bad feeling among the locals.

The house felt right. It was set back from the road and protected by a well-shaped beech hedge. Two big oaks and an ash gave the garden maturity. Roses engulfed the walls of both barns, almost in flower, the "Albertine" more precocious than "New Dawn". The sloping lawns were studded with old apple trees, one or two still in blossom, and all of them promising shade in the summer and bounty in the autumn.

Inside, the rooms spread themselves over the two floors in a pleasingly haphazard fashion. The sitting room had windows on two sides and bookcases in all the right places. Henry could imagine living here and was pleased that Tom and Jane shared his enthusiasm. On leaving, he took the agent aside and offered the asking price plus ten per cent. He said he was a cash buyer and would exchange, without a survey, within two weeks if required. Henry realised he was pushing hard, but the house had been part of Nessa's plan and he wanted to take the good news to her bedside, while there was still time.

The agent called him on Monday morning. If Henry were prepared to offer fifteen per cent more than the asking price and exchange within two weeks, the house was his. The owner would take it off the market.

"I'm confident there will be a few more offers this week with a good chance of a bidding war, but the owner wants to get it over and done with. Against my advice, I should add."

Henry rather liked the agent. On Saturday, he had arrived at the house in a muddy Volvo estate with two child seats strapped to the back seat. His name was Hugo Farrant-Copse and Henry guessed he was in his late thirties. He had thinning blond hair, a country complexion and a languid manner. Henry thought, I would be languid, too, if every new offering I dropped into the housing pool was met with such a feeding frenzy.

"Alright, on the condition that you stop showing the house and we do exchange within two weeks, I'll raise my offer."

Farrant-Copse was delighted.

"I'll inform my client. It's a wonderful house and

close to your family. I'm so pleased it's going to someone with connections in the area."

"Yes, I'm pleased about that, too," Henry said.

31

He closed the door to the yard and locked it behind him. As he expected, there were three parked vehicles – the two flat-beds already loaded for the next day and the Ford van that Morris used. The dog bounded up to him.

"Jock, it's me – good boy."

He laid his hand on the Doberman's flat head and the dog sidled back into the shadows. There was no alarm system. Morris believed that alarm codes were traded in pubs as openly as dud watches and stolen phonecards. He always kept an evil-looking dog around the place and advertised the fact on the yard gates. He would brag that he had never had a break-in.

It was past midnight. What Colin had to do would not take long. In his pocket he had a bag of two-inch masonry nails and picking up a hammer from the yard toolcase he worked his way round the vehicles. He muffled the thwack of the hammer with a folded cloth. There was little noise. On each of the flatbeds he punctured all four tyres at the rear and one of the front tyres. On the van he went for the two back tyres. When a nail pierced the wall of the tyre there was no immediate drama. The tyres were buggered, but they would die a slow death. He was careful to hammer each nail into the shoulder of the tyre where it was impossible to make a repair. It would cost Morris a few grey hairs and a couple of thousand to get things back to rights.

It had been awkward getting the nails in the right place and his arm was hurting. He sat down on the bench outside the shed to recover. Jock ambled over and laid his head on the bench, nuzzling Colin's leg. He scratched the dog's head with the nail that was still in his hand. The animal closed his eyes and squirmed with pleasure. Colin took the hammer and slammed the nail through the dog's skull. It was over before he had thought it through. Jock slid on to the concrete floor, not a squeal, not a yelp, death instantaneous. There was blood where the nail had penetrated and for a few seconds some muscle spasm, but then all was still. Colin looked down with approval. So much for the terror of the yard – Morris' big-time deterrent! He wiped the shaft of the hammer and put it back in the toolcase. He had not planned to kill the dog, but it had worked out well. The tyres would get to Morris in a week or two, but walking in on a dead dog would fuck him up tomorrow. He chuckled at the prospect and let himself out, locking the gate behind him. He dropped his yard key down the first drain he saw.

When he had called in at the yard that afternoon he had sensed that something was wrong. One of the trucks was still out, but two of the boys were busy loading Dave's flatbed for the following day.

"How's it going?"

His greeting had hung in the air, unanswered. When

he opened the office door, Dave was just leaving and they did a little dance on the step to avoid one another. Colin had laughed, but Dave simply stomped off, eyes down.

Morris had been pugnacious.

"The lads don't want you back. And I want an easy life. You can go to the union if you like, but with that bad arm you won't have a leg to stand on."

The bastard had actually laughed at his own joke. "I'm giving you three months' money in lieu of notice – take it or leave it. I don't have to do anything."

He passed an envelope over the desk. "Your cards are in there, too."

"Oh, thanks very much."

"You always were a stupid sod, Colin. Just give me your yard key and piss off."

"Fuck you."

He'd taken the key from his pocket and thrown it on to the desk. It had bounced up and hit Morris just above his left eyebrow, drawing blood. A small satisfaction, but not as pleasing as the knowledge that back at the flat there was a spare yard key hanging from a hook in the kitchen.

As he left the yard, it started raining and the pavements were suddenly slick. He felt conspicuous without a coat. A police car eased out of a side street about a hundred yards ahead of him and turned in his direction. He reached into his pocket for the remaining nails and without breaking step, let them fall to the ground. The police car had stopped – the ignition turned off, whoever was in it obscured by rivulets of rain on the windscreen. An innocent man walking past would be curious and glance into the car, so that's what Colin did, stooping slightly as he passed. He heard the engine start up and the car pull away from the kerb. He did not look back.

He was still half an hour from Ebury Street. He slowed his pace. He wanted time to think things through. He could try another scaffolding firm, but he knew it would be useless. Morris and the boys would put the mark on him. If you were a known diver nobody wanted you up there with them. You were bad luck. They would use his arm as an excuse to keep him out and there was fuck all he could do about it. Which only left Eileen. He would have to be nice to her for a while.

She was asleep when he got in. He did not wake her up.

32

In his earpiece Henry heard familiar folk tunes segue in and out of "Rule Britannia". He recognised the music as the rousing compilation that starts the day on Radio Four, a kind of last night at the Proms early in the morning. Only at this early hour could the B.B.C. get away with such a regular display of flag-waving. For Henry, the music meant the official end of night and was greeted with the relief that all bad sleepers feel when they know it's finally O.K. to get up. But this morning, still thick with sleep, he thought he heard something different. What was it? He must have forgotten to put the lock on the frequency for the medley was being challenged by percussive interference from a neighbouring channel. He would have to retune the bloody thing. From the depth of the pillow he raised his head and realised that the phone was ringing.

"Hello?" His voice was cracked, not fully awake.

"Henry, it's Jack – I'm afraid there's been a turn for the worse. I think you should get the first flight out."

"Well, what – what happened?"

"Just before midnight – she had a stroke. She's in and out of consciousness – and her breathing's bad. They say it could be days, but . . ."

"I'll come as soon as I can. I'll tell Tom."

He sat on the side of the bed as fear took control of his body. He was familiar with the notion of shaking with fright. It was part of his vocabulary, used without examination. Now as the tremors racked him he understood that it was not merely a figure of speech. He was in the grip of an epileptic fear. For twenty minutes his apprehension was tangible – convulsive shivers and chattering teeth seemingly a biological necessity. When they passed he lay on the bed and fell asleep, waking half an hour later. He rang Tom, feeling guilty not to have done it immediately.

Arrangements were soon made. Henry booked the flight tickets on his credit card, grateful for its 24-hour travel service. Tom and Jane were to fly from Norwich by way of Amsterdam. The Burnhams were driving over to pick up Hal.

There were no seats available on any direct flights out of London, but Henry could fly to New York and make a connection to West Palm Beach. It meant a transfer from J.F.K. to LaGuardia by cab, but there was a three-hour window and the man at Amex had been confident it could be done.

In the club lounge, waiting for the flight to be called, Henry studied his fellow travellers. They were for the most part business people. Identified as such, not by their clothes, for neither gender wore business suits these days – instead they dressed in baggy jeans or jogging suits; clothes for the journey not the destination. No, what gave them away was their collective need to be productive. All around him, the laptops were out and the mobiles busy.

"Tell him, I'll email him from the plane."

"Judy, I'm in the lounge, could you get Simon Clark's girl to wire the bank's proposal to my hotel in New York?"

"Donald? It's Philip – I should be with you by 3.00. They'll be calling the flight in fifteen minutes."

Henry closed his eyes and thought of Nessa.

He had once taken a photograph of her as she slept in front of the television. There had been a lamp on a small chest by the arm of her chair and in its light she had looked flawless, like a young girl. He had sat watching her for a long time. It had been a few days after he had followed her to the flat of her lover and before she had confessed. He had felt a great tenderness for her. He had gone into his study for his camera. He had worried that the flash would wake her, but she did not move. When the film was developed the flash had bleached out the charitable lighting and also his forgiveness. He had destroyed the photograph, but not, apparently, the memory.

On the plane he sat next to a young man who had quickly assembled a makeshift office on his tray. When he stood up to take off his sweater, Henry saw from the legend on the back of the T-shirt that he worked for Lehman Brothers and in 1998 had played golf in Hawaii. Henry opened his book and angled his body away from his neighbour. Only once in forty years of business travel had he allowed himself to be drawn into a conversation with the person sitting next to him. On that occasion he had found himself beside an attractive young woman on an overnight flight back from Los

Angeles. They had talked for hours before getting some sleep. The woman's husband had met her in the arrivals lounge and she had introduced him to Henry.

"I hope you don't mind, but I've just spent the night sleeping with your wife," Henry had quipped.

The man had been frosty.

"What did you expect?"

Henry had been surprised at Nessa's reaction when he had told her. "Oh come on, it was just a joke."

"Or a wish," she had said.

33

Jack sat by Nessa's bed hoping for company.

Henry had called three hours ago on his way to LaGuardia. It would be at least another hour before he'd get to the hospital. Tom and Jane had just landed in Miami. It would take them forty-five minutes to clear the airport and then a good hour's drive. He was worried that none of them would arrive in time.

Nessa lay on her back, her head supported by two firm pillows. It was cool in the room and a light, cellular blanket covered her body, but she was far from peaceful and had worked the blanket loose, so that Jack could see the flat planes of her body beneath the gown. Her limbs twitched and jerked. Even more unsettling, the steady rattle of her breathing was regularly punctuated by a guttural cry. Jack was concerned that she was in pain and had called the nurse.

"It's nothing, Jack – it's only the body shutting down. She doesn't feel anything – the brain's doing just enough to keep her breathing. It's pushing the blood around, but nothing more. There's no pain now."

That must be true. They had taken her off the morphine drip yesterday. Didn't want to waste it, he supposed.

"Is it right that hearing is the last thing to go?"

"I don't know, Jack, but you talk to her if you want. She was the nicest lady, always liked to talk."

He noticed the use of the past tense.

She fixed the blanket and left, telling him to call her if there was any change in Nessa's breathing.

And so Jack began an impromptu performance for an audience of one. He would receive no notices and would never talk of it, though over the years, in the presence of Henry, he was often tempted.

At first he talked about her house. He'd been over there that morning. Everything was fine, he said. He had put flowers in the kitchen. There was food in the refrigerator for Tom and Jane. They would be here soon. And he had swept the deck, because he knew she didn't like sand in the living room.

"And the ocean, Nessa – you should see the ocean today. It's beautiful, so peaceful."

He walked to the window. Two nurses were standing in the deep shade of a paradise tree. The tips of their cigarettes glowed in the shadows. One of them threw her stub on to the worn grass. They were young with slender arms. He opened and quickly closed the window as the sound of their laughter drifted in on the tepid air.

"You know something? I never saw the ocean until I was eighteen. We lived in Richmond, Indiana – a long way from the coast, and my father wasn't a curious man."

He tried to recall his father's face. He could see the thin moustache and the high forehead, but everything in between was blurred.

"The truth is, getting cancer was the most adventurous thing my dad ever did. He would drive in the middle of the day with his headlights on. I don't think he had ever thought of going to the ocean. 'Why?' he would have said.

"The summer he died, I hitched to L.A. My first beach was Santa Monica. Not a bad start, wouldn't you say?"

He turned back from the window and saw that Nessa had worked one arm free from the blanket. She was fretful, her breathing even more agitated. He hurried over and held her hand.

"It's alright, Nessa darling. It's Henry, I'm here now."

He stopped.

He had surprised himself. It had been instinctive; this playing to the audience, this desire to give the audience what it wanted. Without thinking he had adopted Henry's accent and cadence. It was yet another voice-over against the clock; something he had spent twenty years perfecting.

Nessa's breathing had quietened. She was peaceful. His instinct had been right; she had been hanging on for Henry.

"I love you, Nessa."

There was no reaction.

"I always have."

He could not quite bring himself to give Henry a clear run.

"Even if I didn't always let you know."

He wanted to work in something about the last few weeks – how special they had been; how he regretted that he had not been more of a dancer, that he had wasted so much time – all the things he imagined Henry would say. He wanted it to be the authentic, regretful Henry, but Jack couldn't bring himself to utter the words. He had grown to like Henry, but this was a time for love, not penitence. He disliked the kind of self-regarding, miserable guilt that Henry carried around with him. Fuck Henry, why isn't he here now to make his own sweet speeches?

He could mimic Henry's voice, but he couldn't *be* Henry; he could never do Henry's cool.

From the reams of dialogue in his actor's memory, came a line. Not the best line, not nearly the best, but the only one that surfaced. It had a kind of legitimacy, he thought. When Henry came over, had he not met Nessa on the beach? Wasn't that where their reconciliation had begun?

He spoke softly, close to her ear.

"You know, I used to live like Robinson Crusoe, shipwrecked among eight million people. Then, one day I saw a footprint in the sand – and there you were."

Had he gone too far? He looked anxiously at Nessa's face, fearing a slight curl of the lips or a narrowing of the eyes. There was nothing. In her prime she would have snorted with disdain.

She would probably have recognised the line. It was from the film *The Apartment*, where Jack Lemmon has just dished up spaghetti on a tennis racket to Shirley MacLaine.

He dropped the accent. "Nessa, I'm so sorry."

He felt ashamed. He bent down to kiss her cheek but found her lips instead. He was close enough to hear the silence when she stopped breathing.

34

When Henry rang, Mrs Abraham had been sitting on the stairs, recovering from a near mishap. She had been changing a light bulb in one of the wall lights on the half-landing. A tricky job, because even with a stepladder, she could not actually see the socket and had to guide the bulb into its bayonet fixing by feel. She had leaned a little too far over and the ladder had wobbled. She had steadied it, but the incident had unnerved her and she had climbed down from the ladder leaving the bulb still loose in the lamp bowl. I'll do it later, she thought.

On the phone, Henry had been direct.

"I'm sorry to tell you, Peggy, that Nessa died yesterday afternoon."

He had never called her Peggy before and his familiarity stunned her as much as did his news. She could not think of what to say and waited for him to continue.

"I missed her."

"Of course, you do. I will, too."

"By about an hour – I missed being there by about an hour."

"Oh, I see."

"Jack was there. He said she never came out of the coma – just slipped away."

Mrs Abraham had been merciful.

"Well, you couldn't have got there any quicker, Mr Cage."

"No, I suppose not."

There was a pause while both of them remembered their disagreement about Henry's premature return to London.

When he spoke again, he was brisker.

"Tom and Jane are coming back on Thursday after the cremation, but I'll stay on for a week or two to sort things out. I'll let you know my plans. Everything alright there?"

"Oh yes, Mr Cage, everything's normal here."

But it did not feel normal. Mrs Abraham, never a shirker, knew that the day's work was over.

She wandered into the dining room. How many times had she helped Nessa get this room ready for a dinner party? Always fun it was. The dining table was painted light grey with a dark-grey edging. It was Swedish, from a shop on the King's Road.

"Henry would have preferred something more formal, but I can't abide brown wood," she had said to Peggy when the table was delivered. They had laughed together at the foolish notions of men. (Though Mrs Abraham's chuckles had been diplomatic. In the front room at home, she had a mahogany dining table – paid for over three years on the never-never and much cherished.)

On feast days, and when needed, she would help

Nessa bring down two extra leaves from the loft and the painted table could seat eighteen with plenty of room for elbows.

In Mrs Abraham's last job they would bring out the best candlesticks and napkin rings and the silver birds from Asprey's. But that was never Nessa's style.

"It's not a state banquet, is it, Peggy? Just friends for supper – let's have some fun."

At one summer party, she had put twelve jugs of sweet peas on the table, interspersed with tall honey-coloured candles. Mrs Abraham had helped serve that night and she would never forget the warm, perfumed air.

When Tom was very little that's what Nessa had called him, she remembered. "How is my sweet pea, then?" she would trill as she bent over the cot.

Taking her time, Mrs Abraham went from room to room. It was still Nessa's house; that's what was nice. There had been no division of the spoils at the time of the divorce. Nessa had taken nothing and Henry had been content to leave things as they were. Nessa might be dead in Florida, but she lived on here in this house in Chelsea.

Cheered by the memory of good times, she went back downstairs to make herself a cup of tea. She would think of Nessa not as dead, but still in Florida, no different really to the last few years. Now, if Mr Cage were to bring a new lady into the house, a lady who doubtless would want to make changes, well then, things would be different. She would have to consider her position, but until then, no need to do anything drastic.

She was halfway through her *Daily Mail* when the doorbell rang. She had been reading her horoscope and the forecast of the loss of a loved one had made her cry.

"Who is it?" she asked on the intercom.

"It's Detective Sergeant Cummings and a colleague."

"Mr Cage is away."

"It's you we'd like to see, Mrs Abraham, if you have a minute?"

Mrs Abraham remembered the policeman. Old-school, she had thought with approval; a solid man with shoulders that filled his jacket, and a nice, straightforward way about him.

"Give me a moment."

Before she went to the door she dried her eyes, put her cup and saucer into the back sink and tucked the *Daily Mail* into the linen drawer. Through the peephole she saw the detective with a uniformed policewoman.

"I don't know how I can help, but come in – we can talk in the kitchen."

They sat around the table. Mrs Abraham offered them coffee, but they said they'd just had one.

"Are you alright, Mrs Abraham? You look as though you've been crying."

"It's Mrs Cage – she died yesterday in Florida. Mr Cage just rang to tell me. She had cancer. Oh . . ."

The policewoman got her a glass of water.

"I'm sorry to hear that. We won't keep you long." Cummings was soothing. He must be used to bad news, she thought.

"I think we may have a lead on Mr Cage's vandal.

Nothing we can act on yet, but I was hoping you could help us with an identification."

He unzipped his document case and laid a photograph on the table.

It was in black and white and larger than the holiday snaps that Mr Abraham took on their annual trip to Mijas. She thought that she had come out better than usual. True, her eyes were wide open with surprise and her mouth was forming a perfect "O", but it was a more becoming look than the frozen smile her husband invariably captured after his careful posing and painstaking wait for the light. She could not help thinking that she looked like the lady of the house, just leaving for a spot of lunch.

"As soon as I saw it, I thought that's Mr Cage's house and that's Mrs Abraham at the door. Do you remember it being taken?"

"Yes, I do. I was just leaving – about lunchtime it was – and as I opened the door they were taking pictures. Two of them – it was the girl who had the camera; she said she liked the garden."

Remembering the Polaroids she heard herself adding.

"Pretty little thing."

"Yes, we've met the girl."

He took another photograph from the case, smaller than the first.

"Was this the man she was with?"

This time it was a more official-looking picture. One of the ones you see pulled out of filing cabinets in police series on the telly. Or these days, clicked up on a screen. It was a man's face against a plain background.

"That's him, but he's older now."

She struggled to remember. There was something else about him that day – what was it?

"Oh, that day, in the garden, one of his arms was in plaster, in a sling."

"Thank you, Mrs Abraham, that was helpful."

She was still examining the photograph, reluctant to hand it back.

"How did you get it?"

"We came across it by accident. We went to see a man about a dog and there it was."

Mrs Abraham smiled at a sudden memory. "My father used to say that when he didn't want to let on. Well, I understand – policemen need to guard their secrets."

"Not only policemen, Mrs Abraham."

He said it evenly, but her knowledge of the Polaroids gave it the force of an accusation that needed to be batted away.

"That's a truth, if ever there was one."

Cummings stood up. "Tell Mr Cage to get in touch when he comes back. And please tell him I'm sorry for his loss."

35

Henry was surprised how easy it had been to arrange a non-religious ceremony. In England, he was sure there would have been pressure to include a few prayers, but here the strictures were more temporal. A notice on the door of the crematorium requested visitors not to wear shorts or sleeveless T-shirts.

The funeral director had officiated and there had been readings from Henry, Jane and Tom. Jack had not wanted to read, but he had made himself responsible for the music. In the hospice, he and Nessa had chosen the tracks and the running order.

The service had been, in effect, a concert with readings. For the committal of the coffin, Nessa had selected "Waltz for Debby" by Bill Evans. Henry had suppressed a chortle, but not well enough to escape the notice of Nessa's cousin from Baltimore, who forever more would think of him as a heartless bastard.

When the will was read the next day, it had been straightforward.

Nessa had left the house with all its furnishings to Tom, with the hope that he and Jane would continue to use it as a holiday home. She had set up a fund to pay for its maintenance and another for her grandchildren's education, confident that Hal would soon have company. She had given her jewellery to Jane.

To "Dear Jack, my friend and carer", she left $50,000, exclusively for the care, protection and eventual replacement of his Impala station wagon.

To Henry, she left all her letters, diaries, scripts, tapes, gardening books and photograph albums. She had packed them into three of her mother's old steamer trunks.

When Tom and Jane returned to England, Henry spent most of his time at Nessa's house. The trunks were lined up in the study. He circled them for days, nervous of what he would find inside. He assumed some of her diaries would be painful, and he knew there would be photographs not only of the life they had enjoyed together, but also of the life he had rejected: pictures of the infant Hal, of Tom and Jane's wedding and of Nessa in the summer gardens of Norfolk. A week after the cremation, the trunks still unopened, he decided to send them to White Horse Farm in Norfolk. He would ask Jack to arrange it.

Undressing that night, he saw that a rash had covered his neck, chest and arms. In the morning, the red blotches had colonised most of his body, even his eyelids and penis. He rang the concierge for an appointment with a doctor. It seemed that there were two options. The hotel had an arrangement with a service providing house calls. The doctors were based in Miami and the call-out would cost $450. The earliest they could send anyone to see him was 5.30 that evening. On the other hand there was a walk-in clinic in Lake Worth, just a twenty-minute drive from the hotel.

Laura on the desk recommended the clinic.

"If you go now, they shouldn't be too busy. They open at 9.00."

The clinic was in a modern brick building set back from the road in a nondescript area of gas stations and junior malls. He walked into an open-plan space with a waiting area to the left of the door. A woman with red hair was at the reception desk working on a computer. She asked Henry to sign in. It was 9.15 and already there was a depressing amount of ink on the form.

"Take a seat, we'll call you."

There were about a dozen people waiting. They looked at him as he sat down and he realised that his reason for being there was self-evident.

"It's not catching," he said.

The man next to him got up and moved to another seat.

Henry opened his book.

"Looks like a heat rash to me."

He looked up. A woman was smiling at him. She was middle-aged in a track-suit top and khaki shorts. Her legs were plump and he saw that one of her knees was pleasantly dimpled. The other was encased in protective padding. A pair of crutches leaned against the back of her chair.

"I'm here about my daughter."

"Oh, I see."

A girl was perched on the seat next to her. Henry guessed she was about fifteen. She was wearing a dancer's black body-suit with flesh-coloured tights over which she wore grey leg warmers. Her hair was scraped back from her forehead in the classical manner. She sat straight-backed on the chair, not pretty, but correct. Every so often, she drew her legs up to her chest and then released them.

The mother shifted in her seat and talked across the room to the receptionist.

"I just want to be sure, hon. Yesterday, she couldn't walk – now today, she wants to go to an audition. I don't want to risk her whole career – there may be a hairline fracture."

In a few moments they are called to the doctor's office. The dancer walks with a wonderful, erect glide and the mother swings along behind on her crutches.

As they leave for the consulting rooms, a stocky man signs in. He is wearing shorts, T-shirt, striped ankle socks and sneakers; the regulation toddler's kit that elderly men revert to in Florida.

He says something to the receptionist about the death of a local stock-car driver. She clucks in sympathy.

"My husband worshipped the man. I have an altar to the guy in my living room."

Twenty minutes later, Henry is called in to see the doctor, a balding, soft-eyed man with an incongruous moustache. He reminds Henry of Edward Elgar, but his name is Dr Fernando Valdes. He asks Henry to loosen his belt, remove his shirt and lie on the bed. The examination is cordial and efficient.

"Are you on any medication?"

"No."

"Well, I don't think it's anything serious. It's an allergy of some kind. We can run some tests, but as you're probably not here for long, there's not much point. I can give you something for the itchiness. The rash should go in two or three days."

He sat at his computer and tapped out a prescription.

"You here on vacation?"

"No, I came over for a funeral.'

"Well, these things can be triggered by stress. Maybe you're allergic to death."

"My wife used to say I was allergic to life."

"I see no evidence of that."

The kindliness of his reply caught Henry off guard. He had not cried since Nessa's death, but now the tears came. He sat on the edge of the surgery bed and fumbled with his shirt buttons. His fingers were wet and his vision blurred and he could not get the buttons into the holes. The doctor placed the prescription and a box of tissues beside him.

"Take your time."

Henry heard the door close.

When he left five minutes later, the doctor was nowhere to be seen. His bill was for $88.

36

"What, they just turned up and rang the doorbell?"

"I told you. I thought you'd forgotten your key. I wasn't to know, was I?"

"Two of them?"

"A detective and a policewoman – they showed their I.D.s and asked for you."

"Why did you let them in?"

"They said they were making enquires about an incident at the yard. I thought you were hurt. I was frightened."

He would not let it go. They'd been over it a hundred times.

"And they asked where I'd been the night before?"

She sighed. "I told them you were here with me – I'm not stupid. All evening and all night, that's what I said."

"And they believed you?"

"I don't know, do I? You tell me what it's about – you're the one that knows."

He had not told her there was a photograph missing from the darkroom. One of them must have asked for the toilet and nosed around. Still, no crime being a garden photographer. Shouldn't have done the dog, though. Morris isn't stupid. He'd have put them straight on to me. But so what? They couldn't prove anything. The missing photograph worried him more.

The next day, he decided to take a look at the house in Chelsea. He had been wondering what Henry had done with the Polaroids. If he had handed them over to the police there was a chance that one of the coppers might have recognised Eileen, but it was a long shot. The pictures had not exactly concentrated on her face. The old perv wouldn't have turned them in, anyhow. More likely, he was still jerking off to them.

He walked without urgency through Sloane Square and up to South Kensington station, where he bought a *Daily Telegraph*. He had been an *Independent* reader once. When they first started, they had given a lot of space to photography – big pictures, across two pages – but like everything else, it had not lasted. When the paper lost its photographic nerve, he had switched to the *Telegraph*. At the yard they called him a Tory wanker, but the truth was, politics didn't come into it. He simply liked a big paper and he'd found there was too much foreign stuff in the *Guardian* and *The Times*.

He took his paper into Dino's next to the station and ordered a coffee and two rounds of buttered toast, well done. He read the sports section first and then the main paper from the back, working up to page three. There were no tit shots in the *Telegraph*, but there was usually a sexy story on page three, in surprising detail for a posh paper. While thumbing through he was stopped by a picture of a pretty woman on the obituaries page. It was not the death of the day, but a smaller, squat space at the bottom of the page. She was laughing, her dark hair windswept and tousled. It looked like she was on a mountain somewhere. Yes, that's what the caption said, "'Nessa Cage on location for *Ladies Above the Timber Line*, her award-winning film about the early women mountaineers." He looked at the headline, VANESSA CAGE. DOCUMENTARY FILM-MAKER. He wondered if there was a connection; it was not a common name, after all. He paused and concentrated on the remaining triangle of toast, burned almost black, as he liked it, and smeared with butter.

Mrs Abraham saw him from Henry's bedroom. She had opened the window that morning to air the room and was just closing up before leaving. He had a newspaper. She noticed he carried it like a gentleman, not rolled up, but folded in half. He had glanced over at the house but had not stopped. She hurried downstairs and rang Cummings at the police station.

"He didn't do anything, just walked by and looked over – but I thought you'd like to know."

"Quite right, Mrs Abraham, thank you for calling. You won't forget to give my message to Mr Cage, will you?"

His dismissive reply puzzled her. She buttoned her raincoat, aware that there was much in the world that escaped her – and happy, for the most part, that it did.

As she locked the front door it crossed her mind that the young man might be hanging around, so she was not entirely surprised to see him as she turned the corner, though she had not expected to see him flat on his back. Her first thought was that he had slipped, her second that he had been mugged for as she drew closer she saw that his hands were up, shielding his eyes.

"Are you alright?"

As he turned his head, she saw that he was holding a small camera.

"Oh, it's you. I'm fine, just trying to get a shot of these blossoms. Always got my camera with me, just in case."

She looked up and saw the white blossom against the blue of the sky. It was like one of the covers of the *Country Life* magazine that Mr Cage got every week.

"It looks lovely," she said.

"That should do it."

He stood up and she saw that he had been lying on his newspaper – the pages spread out like a dustsheet.

"About all they're good for," he said as he gathered up the pages. "Nothing but bad news, is there?"

His jacket had been folded neatly on a low garden wall and before he put it on, he looked it over carefully. There was some brick dust on a sleeve and he gave the jacket a gentle shake. He decided to take a chance.

"Talking of which, I was sorry to read about Mrs Cage. Have you seen the obituary?" He offered her a sheet of his newspaper.

She was startled. "Yes, I have, thank you."

"Well then, I'll find a bin for this lot and I'll be off."

She watched him slip the camera into his pocket and walk up to the Fulham Road. He raised his arm in farewell as he turned the corner. She sat down on the wall, feeling faint. She wanted a cigarette though she had not smoked for seven years. In her handbag she found a cough sweet and sucking it brought the saliva back to her mouth. The young man's recklessness had frightened her. He should not have mentioned Mrs Cage; he was meant to be a stranger who liked gardens.

37

Ed Needy was in Maude's bed. He was worrying about the company's share price.

"Yesterday, it was down another 8p."

Maude lay on her back looking up at the skylight. It was dawn and rain was washing the grime from the glass. I can postpone the window cleaner for another couple of weeks, she thought, before answering.

"Is that significant?"

"Who knows?"

Ed was not yet a rich man. He had arrived at Henry Cage & Partners too late for the initial division of equity and although he had accumulated share options, presently valued at £315,000, he still had almost a year to wait until he could cash in the first tranche. If the share price continued to fall, his money could disappear. He had hoped that with the ousting of Henry, business would boom, but, if anything, the opposite had happened.

Charles had urged patience.

"A company's image is nearly always three years behind the reality," he had said. "We're not suddenly going to get a Toys 'R' Us or a tobacco company at our door, simply because we will now do business with them. It doesn't work like that. Some of them will want to punish us for Henry's fastidiousness and keep us waiting; others are happy where they are – and most of them haven't even heard of us. It will take time, but word will get around, aided and abetted by some strategically placed P.R." He had smiled. "Not in a hurry, are you, Ed?"

It was easy for him to be sanguine. Over the past ten years of a rising market, the partners had sold off blocks of shares at intervals and put the money into bonds or houses in Regency crescents and fashionable shires. It was alright for them – they were home and dry; the company could go belly up and they would still go on enjoying their safe, platinum lives.

Ed sighed, looking up at the rain.

"Why don't they just give me socking great cash bonuses like Goldman Sachs?"

"I guess they want you to feel involved with the company. You know – ownership, the family, belonging."

She was parroting something she had heard Henry say, but it did not console him.

"I'm not temperamentally suited to option schemes. I worry. I call up the share price on my screen twenty times a day. It's a nightmare."

She saw him look at his watch. Any moment now, he would swing out of bed and claim first use of the bathroom. He would be in there for twenty-five minutes, leaving all the towels folded and all the surfaces wiped down. If he had used the loo, the end of the toilet paper would be folded to form an arrow-head. She had never been to his flat, but she imagined it to be a temple to prissiness.

He slept with her once a week on Tuesday nights. (Wednesday being the only day when he did not have a 6.30 a.m. session at the gym.) He was not married, had no regular girlfriend and they were both discreet and undemanding. It was a relationship devoid of drama. He was courteous and considerate, but he obviously did not adore her. It was like living at home; with the bonus of weekly sex. She was surprised to find herself happy with the arrangement. For the moment.

"See you later," he said on his way out.

She went to the window and watched him cross the road. Luckily, his car had not been blocked in.

Ed was on the sixth floor with Charles when she arrived at the office. She made herself a coffee and went into his private meeting room where the newspapers had been left on the table. First thing every morning, she went through the papers for him, highlighting with a yellow marker any items that mentioned the company, their clients, the client's industries or the competition. She also flagged all relevant personnel moves. It was a task that Maude enjoyed and over the weeks she had broadened the range of his reading, marking out social trends, significant awards, deaths and marriages, even the odd bit of gossip about people he might know. He had been appreciative.

The tabloids had not detained her for long that morning and she picked up *The Times* hoping for richer pickings. On the obituaries page she saw a photograph of Henry with his arm around the shoulder of a laughing, dark-haired woman. So that was Nessa; she looked too nice to kick out. Poor Henry. She read the obituary and gave it a yellow frame.

38

On the plane Henry tried to read, but he found he could not concentrate. He put down his book and picked up the in-flight magazine. On the cover was a photograph of Venice. He heard a small bleat of distress and looked around before realising that the sound had come from his own throat. There were only four other passengers in the cabin and they were all sleeping. Nobody had heard his involuntary cry. He looked again at the cover. It was essentially a photograph of a sunset, but in the shadows of the foreground he had recognised a familiar restaurant with its few tables set by the water's edge.

It was a restaurant that he and Nessa had loved. It was the best place in all of Venice to watch the sun go down. Sometimes, while they dined, a cruise ship would glide by, obscuring even the lofty warehouses on the opposite bank of the Giudecca canal. The passengers had a grandstand view of the city and they lined every deck, some of them waving to the diners below. Nessa would always wave in return, but only once had she been able to persuade Henry to respond. He had raised his arm as though he were catching a ball. He remembered her laughter. She had called it a greeting without feeling – no better than a gloved handshake.

The restaurant was owned by a young, married couple. She cooked and he took care of the front of house. The food they served was sublime. At midday, a fisherman docked his small boat just yards from the restaurant's front door and the couple came out to the quay and chose the fish for dinner that night. The menu was hand-written and forever changing. They served either what was fresh from the sea or irresistible in the market.

Henry had once built a business lecture around the restaurant. It had been on one of his favourite themes. He believed that good businesses are an act of will and that the desire to be great has to be constant. Companies do not lose their energy and integrity overnight. They fade by degrees. A small cut here, a compromise there, and before you know it you are running an ordinary outfit.

Quality in any enterprise is always under attack and particularly so during periods of growth. In the lecture, he had shown the restaurant as it was and had then outlined how easily it could have lost its way by making a series of what appeared to be rational management decisions. He had taken his audience through these hypothetical changes – all of them logical, all of them deadly.

Happily, in real life, the restaurant had not changed. It had remained enchanting and unique.

He thought of the last time he and Nessa had been there together. The sky had been heavy with cloud, a storm predicted around midnight. They had the place to themselves and had chosen a table well back from the anticipated turbulence of the water. They had not been seated long before a priest had joined them on the terrace, an elderly man, balding and slim, in dog collar and black suit and clutching a copy of the *New Yorker*. Henry had been intrigued.

When the waiter arrived, it was obvious that the priest was a regular. He was shown to the table next to them.

"He's wearing white socks – how sweet," Nessa said.

The priest had ordered his dinner in Italian, switching to English in mid-sentence. The owner had called him Padre.

The storm had arrived earlier than predicted, a dry storm as it had turned out. At the first sight of lightning the priest had started counting out loud. He had got to eight before the thunder came – a deep rumble and then three sharp explosions, almost overhead.

"God's artillery," he had said, turning his chair to talk to them. "But we must sit tight. It would be a sin to abandon such food."

He had been keen for company.

"I'm American, though my ancestors were a mixed lot. My mother had a place in Venice and I came to live with her when I retired from my ministry. I have been here several years. There are worse fates."

"Where were you before?" Henry had asked.

"First, in Washington and then in New York, where I had many disagreements with Cardinal Spellman."

He had told them he was writing a memoir. He was planning to call it *Thick* because one conservative bishop had once told him that the Vatican had a file this thick of his liberal transgressions. He had opened his hand to show a gap of five inches between his thumb and index finger.

"An apt title, wouldn't you say?"

He had talked of the writers and painters he had known and seemed gratified that he had been criticised by his superiors for his friendships with the rich and famous.

"I love rich people no less fervently than the needy. My only guiding belief has been that the Church should never make anyone cry."

When they got up to leave, he had asked them to say a prayer for an old priest.

Nessa had kissed him on both cheeks and proclaimed it the best dinner she had ever had in Venice – with the best company.

That Sunday, they had attended mass at the Chiesa delle Zitelle, a church not always open, and rarely used by tourists. Apart from themselves, the congregation had consisted of nineteen elderly women and just three men.

Henry had whispered to Nessa, "God gathers first those whom he loves best."

She had replied, "It's not God who gathers the men, it's younger women."

Henry settled back in his seat. Even in memory, Nessa could make him laugh. He closed his eyes and was soon asleep.

39

Henry did not have the look of a grieving man. Careless about eating since Nessa's death, he had become trim and his daily walks on the beach had given him a tan. He felt indecently presentable. Even Mrs Abraham, who had greeted him with tears, had been unable to resist saying, "You look well, anyhow."

They were sitting at the kitchen table. In front of him, in neat stacks, were what seemed to be hundreds of letters. He could see that some of the envelopes were black-edged and on many he recognised the logo of Henry Cage & Partners.

"It looks as though I have a lot to do," he said.

Mrs Abraham had not thought it appropriate to tell Henry of the policeman's visit while he was in Florida, but now she was impatient to give him her news.

"He had a photograph of the garden and me opening the front door. It was taken by this girl who was with the man they think might be responsible for the vandalism." The words tumbled from her.

"I didn't think to tell you when I saw them taking the pictures – must have been a few weeks ago – I mean, people are always taking snaps of this street, aren't they?" She paused for breath. "The detective wants you to ring him."

Henry was amused to see that her face was flushed with excitement.

"Did Cummings have a picture of the man?"

"Yes, an old one, but it was him alright – smart-looking chap."

"I'll get in touch and see what it's all about. Now, I'd better get this suitcase up the stairs."

He was deliberately businesslike.

"If you want to get off early, Mrs Abraham, that would suit me. I didn't sleep on the flight, and could do with a rest. We'll talk some more tomorrow morning."

He was aware of her disappointment as he climbed the stairs. He should have stayed and talked to her. He had remembered to bring her an Order of Service from the funeral, but it was still in his suitcase. He stopped and turned to see her putting on her coat.

"Oh, I should tell you, Peggy, that Nessa wanted me to give you a cheque for £10,000 – from her estate. I'll let you have it when the lawyers are through."

He thought she was going to collapse. Her hand went up to her mouth and she wobbled, but as he came down the stairs she shook her head and bolted through the front door.

Surprisingly, there had been no such request in Nessa's will. Perhaps she knew I would take care of it, he thought.

He went to see Cummings early next morning at Chelsea police station. The interview was more frank than on previous occasions, but not completely so.

"I do recognise the man, yes. I had a run-in with him

on Millennium night. I was pushed into him by the crowd and he kicked and head-butted me."

"And did you ever see him again?"

"Once, in the Sloane Square brasserie."

"Did he see you?"

"He complained about me to the manager. He said I was staring at his girlfriend. I was asked to leave."

"And did you?"

"I was embarrassed. It wasn't true."

The photograph of his house and front garden lay on the table between them. Cummings explained how he had come by it.

"I'm pretty sure he's our man, Mr Cage. His name is Colin Bateman. There's a history of violence. Did Mrs Abraham tell you he was outside your house again last week?"

"No – we haven't had much chance to talk."

"We had him in for a chat and I've warned him off, but that's about all we can do. We can't prove anything. A few weeks ago he hammered a masonry nail through a dog's skull to even a score, but I can't prove that either – his girlfriend was quick with an alibi. But sooner or later, he'll slip up – they all do – and then we'll have him."

He was a decent man and Henry felt the need to reassure him.

"I'm sure you will, but I've decided to sell the house. I'm going to live in Norfolk. My son and his wife are there already – and my grandson."

Cummings noted the softening of Henry's voice at the mention of a grandson.

"Well, in the meantime, let's hope our man takes my warning to heart. I wish you a quick sale and a more peaceful life in the country."

He stood up and held out his hand. The interview was over.

As Henry left, he felt for the envelope in the inside pocket of his jacket. He had intended to hand over the Polaroids to Cummings, but the need had not arisen and he was thankful to be spared the embarrassment of an explanation.

He decided to walk home via the John Sandoe bookshop, just off the King's Road. Like all the bookshops he loved, it was small and intimate, a miracle of compression. Books were everywhere. On the staircase to the paperback room, stacks of books were kept on the treads, leaving little room for going up and down. (It was rumoured that no-one with a shoe size of over 10 had ever made it up there.)

The shop seemed to order only books that Henry wanted to read and he quickened his step, eager to see what treasures were on the tables. The store was busy and he browsed for half an hour, careful as he moved from one pile of books to another not to hurry the customer next to him. Good manners are a given in bookshops. "I don't suppose you have a copy of . . ." The tone is invariably considerate. Between a book's covers there may be passion, bile, mayhem or murder, but in the quiet spaces where it awaits its fate (either acceptance or indifference) all is calm. For Henry, bookshops had always been restorative, and buoyed by his visit he bought Thom Gunn's latest book of poems and left.

It was just after 2.00 and the King's Road was busy. A young woman cut across him and darted through the open doors of Body Shop. He recognised her as the head-butter's girlfriend and from her haste he imagined she was late back from lunch. He followed her into the shop only to see her disappear through the staff door. He waited, affecting an interest in a display of exfoliating sponges. The packaging informed him that they had been "ingeniously recycled from plastic bottles". When he looked up, she was back in the shop, standing behind the till, wearing a black Body Shop T-shirt. He could not help noticing how beautifully her breasts conformed to the images he had in his inside pocket. He turned and walked towards her.

40

Unlike his parents, Hal believed in heaven.

One morning before class, Miss Martha had told him that his grandma had been in so much pain that God had wanted her in heaven where he could take care of her. This had seemed sensible to Hal. In his world, the grown-ups looked after the children and God looked after the grown-ups.

After school, he had asked his mother if she, too, thought that Grandma was in heaven.

"Perhaps she is."

Jane had been anxious to comfort her son, but true to her own atheism, unwilling to be more than non-committal. She would have liked to tell Hal the truth: his grandmother had been ill and had died, that he would never see her again – anywhere.

Tom thought such honesty needlessly brutal and had cut in with a warning glance.

"Of course she's in heaven – definitely."

But it had been too late. Hal knew what his mother's "perhaps" meant. It meant we might not go to the beach. It meant he might not have an ice cream. It meant that Grandma might not be in heaven.

When he thought about it, he was troubled. Miss

Martha was a teacher, so he ought to believe her, but he also knew that his mother did not lie. It was very confusing – if Grandma Nessa was not in heaven, then where was she?

Over the next few days he was quieter than usual, content to curl up on his father's lap after school. At the weekend, for the first time in months, he wet his bed.

In the past, Tom had always known how to help his son through the spasms of sadness that occasionally laid him low. At two, the boy's grief had been easy to spot and simple to remedy. When thwarted, Hal would fall to the floor, face down and mute, a tiny package of frozen misery. Sometimes Tom would lie beside him, saying nothing, prone as the boy himself, waiting it out. Before long, Hal would turn on his side and pull his father's hair, a signal that the sulk was over.

At other times, Tom would step over his son and disappear into the kitchen, saying he had things to do. Inevitably, he made a noise, several noises, in fact. The double click of two tumblers hitting the kitchen counter, the cushioned clatter of the refrigerator door being opened and closed and then the hiss of escaping bubbles as Tom pulled the tab on a can of cola. Wonder of wonders, Hal would be back on his feet, grinning at the kitchen door.

But this present sadness was different – different, too, from the misery of sickness. Tom had seen Hal passive and bewildered by fever; had lain with him throughout the night, gratuitously inhaling the Karvol on his son's pillow. These things he had known, and known how to handle, but what ailed his son now was loss and he did not know how to help.

The bed-wetting stopped, but Hal's vitality did not return. Tom and Jane tried diversions.

At the Burnhams' for Sunday lunch, they had asked one of Hal's cousins to bring his new puppy, a white Parsons terrier with one eye ringed in black. The dog's cheerfulness was contagious. Its floppy running had made Hal laugh, but in the car going home he was pensive.

"When is Grandpa Henry coming?" he said.

"Next weekend. He's driving up to see the new house."

He decided he would ask his grandfather about Nessa. He would know where she was.

Henry arrived on Saturday, one day after Nessa's trunks. He had asked Tom to drive over to White Horse Farm and take delivery. In the boot of the Mercedes, Henry had packed a rolled-up futon, a sleeping bag and the small video-playing television from his bedroom in London. He planned to open the trunks, play some of the tapes, and sleep one night in the empty house. He stopped at the supermarket in Swaffham and bought what he needed for his short stay.

It was late June and the garden was in its full glory. He saw that Tom had been over to cut the grass. It all looked perfect. In years to come, he would discover that White Horse Farm was blessed. Lying in a shallow valley and sheltered by woods to the northeast, it escaped the worst of the winter winds and summer came early. It was a garden where roses thrived and fruit always ripened. By September, the vines on the south-facing walls would be heavy with grapes. But even on that first morning, before he had absorbed the full extent of his luck, he knew that leaving London for this house would be no hardship.

He found the keys where Tom had left them in the barn and decided to walk the boundaries before going inside. From the vegetable garden, part of an upper lawn that had once been a tennis court, Henry paused to look down at the house, sprawling like a contented cat in the morning sunshine. It seemed a far cry from the King's Road.

"You know who I am, don't you?"

It had been done on impulse. Seeing her, it had seemed the right thing to do. He had wanted to get rid of the damn things and she should know the kind of man she was protecting.

She had nodded.

"These were put through my letterbox a few weeks ago. Don't open them here. No-one else has seen them."

He had put the envelope on the counter.

"I'm sorry. I really am."

On the street, he had felt elated. The thing was over, done with. He was leaving London and if the girl had any sense she would leave Colin whatever-his-name-was and get her life back to normal. The sooner he put the Chelsea house on the market the better. He would see to it after the weekend.

Now he was here in the clean, wholesome air of Norfolk. He walked down the grassy slope towards the house.

Nessa's trunks had been meticulously organised. There was an index of the contents in each trunk and each item – be it diary, file, script, photograph album or tape – had been individually labelled.

He looked at the tapes first. In her films she had always been the on-camera interviewer. It had been one of her strengths. Each documentary had been a personal testament. It was her voice you heard, her face you saw, and her truth that filled each frame.

In 1980, she had been allowed into a women's prison and *The Girls Inside* had chronicled the lives of the inmates of Cell Block C over a period of three years. It was the series that had made her name. Nessa had persuaded the commissioning editor to let her shoot the films in black and white, using 16-mm film. This was considered quite a coup, for film was no longer the format of choice at the B.B.C. Tape was cheaper and more versatile, but Nessa had wanted film for its extra quality and had fought, charmed and cajoled to get it.

She had been honest in her portrayal of prison life and much of the footage had been bleak, but by using extreme close-ups and long takes, she had created a visual style that raised the films above conventional fly-on-the-wall reportage.

Many of the inmates had been young and Nessa had captured their vulnerability. One storyline had followed a woman who had given birth in the prison, her confinement being all the more moving for being literal. The tone of the films had been established early with the opening titles. They were played against shots of the exercise yard at dawn. Nessa had scattered birdseed on the ground and on the sills of the barred windows. As the prisoners slept in their cells, birds were seen flying in and out of the yard at will. It had been an obvious piece of imagery, but she had been lucky, for the night before the filming it had started to snow and the flakes were still falling as the camera turned. She had removed the lens hood and allowed the snow to gradually blur the glass, like a curtain of tears.

Henry had suggested that she use a track of Bill Evans playing "Danny Boy" as background music to the title sequence. The piece had been recorded in April 1962, the first time Evans had been near a piano for nine months. He had been mourning the death in a road accident of Scott LaFaro, the bass player in the first Bill Evans trio. The April recording had been planned as an introduction to the trio's enforced new line-up, but this particular track turned out to be about the past. It was plainly a lament for Scott.

In the recording you can feel the grief as Evans slowly introduces the familiar melody. So halting is his progress, you wonder if he is going to make it. Time after time, you feel he has held back the note far too long, and then – and then – just as you know for certain he has lost all continuity, the note falls, as right and as wanted as the delayed thrust in lovemaking.

The mix had been perfect and Nessa had fought hard to extend the opening sequence so that it could end on a natural break for the music. The sequence ran for two minutes and thirty-four seconds, an indulgence, but the softly falling snow and the music had moved in unison and the effect had been heartbreaking. He watched the films for three hours, fast-forwarding to the sections where Nessa appeared on screen. At 2.00 he made a sandwich and went out into the garden. Swallows swooped in and out of the barns.

In the afternoon he started on the home movies. They were as polished as her documentaries, expertly edited with sync. sound and full effects. Watching them, he had felt like a man locked out of his own house. Every frame had hurt. One beach sequence of Hal attempting cartwheels to the corny drum roll of the circus tent had sent him out into the garden for air.

He was still outside when Tom and Hal arrived.

"Can I leave him with you for an hour? He's been nagging me all day about coming over."

"Of course, I could use a bit of company, especially Hal's."

They went into the front room. The tape was still running and the boy quickly squatted down in front of the television set. Henry, in his ignorance, was worried that he was sitting too close to the screen but said nothing.

"Do you remember that holiday?"

"Oh, yes."

When it was over, Hal had pleaded to watch one more tape. Henry chose one of the Norfolk series, a film of a boat trip to watch the seals basking out on Blakeney Point. Hal had cried out with pleasure when Tom had taken over the camera and filmed Nessa taking off her Wellington boots. She had solemnly turned them upside down. There must have been two litres of North Sea in each boot.

Afterwards, Hal and Henry had sat on the high bank in the garden, sharing a plate of jam sandwiches. They were still there, talking, when Tom arrived to take Hal home.

In the days that followed, Hal resumed the walks with his father. He did not know why he felt happier, he just did.

41

Eileen took her time leaving Colin. For three weeks she lived with him as though nothing had happened. She never mentioned the Polaroids and tried to keep out of his way. She volunteered to work three Sundays in a row.

"Two of the girls are sick," she told him.

He walked away.

"They asked if I could help out," she said.

After that, he had been silent for days, coming out of his darkroom only to eat or use the loo.

She had been dreading sex, but it had been surprisingly easy to avoid. He hadn't shown any interest, and when he finally did come near her, she said she was not in the mood and he backed off. Despite herself, she felt annoyed that he had not put up more of a fight.

She had told them at work that she was having trouble with an ex-boyfriend who had turned into a bit of a stalker and they had agreed to transfer her to a branch in north London.

"If a man comes in asking for me, you know nothing, right?"

She had found a flat share through a friend. It was in Highbury, a short bus ride from the new shop and far away from Ebury Street.

She phoned her mum and said that Colin had become weird and moody and she was leaving him.

"If he gets in touch, tell him you don't know where I am."

"Well, I don't, do I? Where are you?"

"With a friend – I'm alright – don't worry."

It was done. She was all set, ready to go.

Twenty-four days after Henry had walked into Body Shop, Eileen walked out on Colin. She left an envelope on the table containing the three Polaroids cut up into small pieces.

Colin would twig where the photographs had come from, but so what? She wanted him to know why she had left. The pictures were meant to be private. Just for them, he had said. When the bloke from Chelsea had come into the shop he had seemed quite nice, but later she had noticed the thumbprints all over the pictures. What did that make her? She was not some low-life porn queen. She didn't give a fuck what happened to him – or Colin. She was out of it – she was gone.

As it turned out, covering her tracks proved to be unnecessary. Colin never tried to find her. True, she might have made him some money, but she was never going to be big-time and, anyhow, his anger was directed elsewhere. He was surprised that Henry had given Eileen the Polaroids. It had served no purpose other than malice. Not a nice thing to do. Not a nice thing at all.

That evening, he put the envelope with the torn pictures into a drawer and cleaned the flat. He put fresh sheets on the bed and opened the windows. Eileen, for all her looks, had been a bit of a slut in the home-making department. Running his finger around the plughole of the bathroom sink he had pulled out a coil of her hair, gritty now with a residue of soap and tooth-paste. He dropped it into the loo before washing his hands. In the bathroom cabinet, he found a pile of used cotton buds. He picked them up with a tissue.

When night came he slept diagonally in his bed for the first time in a year. He relished the space, the absence of her.

Three weeks later he was feeling less calm. His redundancy money was running out and as he had feared, there were no scaffolding jobs on offer. Morris had indeed put the word out. At Metro, one of the bigger companies, where Colin had worked in the past, the boss had made it personal.

"I couldn't hire you, Colin, could I? See, I'm a bit of an animal lover. You know what I mean?"

"Yeah, well thanks for nothing."

"I'd be thinking about a change of career, if I were you."

With nothing to do, Colin walked the streets with his camera. He had made money in the past selling London scenes to the picture libraries. It was a hit-and-miss business, but sometimes you got lucky.

On the third morning he was sitting in a Starbucks on the Brompton Road. Through the window he was watching two young women at an outside table. One of the girls was talking. She was a wispy thing, long in the face with a bad complexion. He was not tempted to take her picture; the girl was worse than ordinary, a complete zero. That is, until she stopped talking. Even before her friend had uttered a word, the weedy girl had prepared her face for listening, opening her mouth wide in astonishment. She had held the pose as if for a dentist, her mouth a gaping hole as large as a lemon. Colin had time to shoot off a roll of film before she closed it. He knew that he had something. The girl's freaky eagerness to please would be there in the photographs for all to see. He left, impatient to be in his darkroom.

Back home, he checked his messages.

"Colin, what's up man? It's Geoff – Geoff White. That tanning brochure you sent me a few weeks back with your girl in it – well, I've got a job for her. I reckon it could be worth six grand or thereabouts – a calendar number. A bit of travel and all. Call me, O.K.?"

Colin put the phone down, forgetting all about the darkroom and the open-mouthed girl, thinking only of the pervert in Chelsea who had cost him money.

42

Crompton and Partners claimed in their literature that they were London's most contemporary estate agency. Walking into their Chelsea office, Henry could see that it was certainly true of the staff. No-one was over thirty and, without exception, they were all good-looking.

Helen, blonde, exquisite and a "senior negotiator", guided Henry to her desk. It was uncluttered; nothing on it but the very latest laptop – as slim as a January magazine. She opened it, ready for work.

"I want to sell my house in Brentwood Place."

"One of my favourite streets – like the country in London. I love it."

"The thing is, I want to sell it quietly. No advertising, no editorials" – Henry waved a hand at her computer – "no hoop-la."

"Sometimes it's necessary, but not in this case. We have a waiting list for Brentwood Place."

She agreed a time to come and see the house that afternoon. She said they had sold a property in the street not long ago and the buyer had paid well over the asking price. As they shook hands, she remained businesslike. He had been expecting a winning smile, but it seemed that was not the contemporary thing to do.

Later, after her inspection of the house, they agreed an asking price and arranged that viewings would be in the afternoons only. Henry wanted the house immaculate, but preferred that Mrs Abraham, the architect of that perfection, was out of the way.

The house was sold in a week to a Russian businessman who could pay cash. Exchange and completion were guaranteed in four weeks.

"I'll stay until you go, if that's alright. You'll need a hand getting everything ready for the movers."

"That's kind of you, Mrs Abraham. What will you do after, I mean, will you look for another job?"

"My afternoon lady wants me to do more hours. She's always on about it. There's so much ironing, what with the children, but I never wanted to leave while you were here, not while Mrs Cage's things were still about . . ."

She could not go on and hurried down to the laundry room. He knew that she had been close to Nessa, but it had never occurred to him that she had stayed on after the divorce by choice, that there had been other options. He wondered if she might have preferred spending more time with her afternoon lady in a home with bustle and children. He imagined her coming into his house each day, not even the tick of a clock to welcome her.

That morning as she left, he gave her the promised cheque. She made a move as if to hug him, but gave him her hand instead. He was surprised by the roughness of her skin.

Later, he played the piano for the first time in weeks; a farewell concert for the house, its gardens and its memories.

43

Henry's bedroom was at the front of the house. He and Nessa had always slept with the window open, the window locks positioned so that he could push the sash up four inches before they came into play.

In ordinary times this allowed for a sufficient airflow, but this spring the Banksia rose had put on so much growth that the air had to fight its way through a thick screen of foliage. He had agreed with Mark and Marco, the gardeners who came once a week, that they should discuss cutting the rose back with the new owner when he arrived. He remembered the man's entrancement when he had first seen the green and yellow of the rose in bloom.

"My racing colours," he had said with satisfaction.

Henry knew from the agent that the man from Moscow planned to update the house and put in air-conditioning. More efficient, Henry conceded, than two raised window locks, but he hated the thought that the house was to be ripped apart. He wished now that he had sold it to a downsizing couple from the country, exiles from Wiltshire or Dorset who now wanted to be near their children and the London hospitals. They would have moved in and changed nothing.

The night before the removal men were due to arrive for the two days of packing and loading, Henry lay awake in his bed. He regretted his decision not to trim back the rose. The small amount of air that did seep into the room was warm, and it made Henry more restless than usual. The talk show on the radio was no help. Once again, they were debating abortion. Pro or con, the callers were all bigots. Prejudices were aired, but minds were never changed. Instead of sheep, he counted the number of times each caller said "you know" – surely the most virulent virus ever to attack the English language? He gave up when Mary from the Isle of Wight managed to say it thirty-eight times in her short but fractured call.

It was 2.30. He removed his earpiece and propped himself up against his two pillows. Sometimes a change of position would send him to sleep. He looked around the room. Every object reminded him of Nessa. Soon they would all be gone, bundled off to Norfolk – to a house that she had never seen.

He began to take an inventory.

1. The bed, the most comfortable they had ever had. Bought from Heal's, it had been too big for the staircase and had been hoisted in through the window.
2. The walnut chest, bought together in the Pimlico Road. Nessa had used the two top drawers. They had been empty since the day she had moved out.
3. The oil painting of three bathers by Bernard Meninsky. It had been a Christmas present to themselves the year the business had first shown a profit.

They had hung it opposite the bed instead of a mirror. "Better bodies," Nessa had said.

4. The Venetian mirror by the door. He had bought it from a dealer in Marylebone, an elderly lady with a heart of flint. At home, Nessa had seen immediately that it was not as described on the invoice, but had said it didn't matter because, fake or not, it was genuinely beautiful.
5. On the mantelpiece, a small wooden box with a sliding lid. On top of the box, he saw the triangle of lettered cards. He knew the words by heart. WILL NOT FALL APART.

He had found the box in one of Nessa's trunks and brought it back to London, wanting it by his side. She must have bought it from the owner of the cottage, he thought – Nessa would never steal . . . His eyes felt heavy. I can't let the movers pack that, it can go in the car with me . . .

Somewhere between wakefulness and sleep, he became aware of a small rhythmic sound.

It was a back and forth kind of noise, two regular, repeated notes. He went to the window, but the rose blocked his view. The sound was muted but insistent and it was coming from the front garden.

He put on his dressing gown. Halfway down the stairs, he stopped and went back for his baseball bat, fearing an intruder. In the hallway, the noise seemed to have stopped. Probably only a rodent gnawing on a kill, he thought, but he'd check anyway. He opened the door quietly.

The sound was back. Close to, it had more of a rasp to it – hee-haw, hee-haw. He stepped out on to the path. He looked left, towards the source of the sound. There was a dark, huddled figure at the base of the rose, too big to be a woman.

He caught a glint from the blade of a curved hand-saw. Shit, someone was sawing through the trunk of the Banksia.

"What the hell are you doing? That rose is thirty years old, for God's sake!"

He heard himself with dismay. Even *in extremis*, he sounded like a park-keeper.

The man turned and got to his feet. Henry recognised him even before he had straightened.

"Not any more, it isn't."

The man was smiling. He took a step towards Henry.

"You're mad, the police know all about you."

"What's the offence, Mr Cage?"

He moved closer.

"Destruction of a rose bush? What's that – seven days' community service?"

He took another step towards Henry, the saw in his hand.

"And anyhow, I wasn't here. You never saw me, right?"

Another step. The smile had gone. The words now were hissed out in anger.

Henry stepped back and instinctively widened his stance. He kept his eyes on the saw in Bateman's hand.

"I hear you dropped off some photographs?"

Bateman moved closer.

"You keep your fucking nose out of my business, you hear?"

He was close enough for Henry to smell the sap on the saw.

"You hear me? Do you?"

Henry saw the handsaw rise and swung the baseball bat, hoping to parry the blow.

He was taller than Colin and the arc of his swing brought the bat down on to Colin's shoulder where it ricocheted upwards, smashing into the skull just above the left ear.

Bateman went down, still clutching the saw.

Henry stood for a moment, breathing hard, and then went back into the house.

He made a 999 call, asking for an ambulance and then the police.

He waited for them outside on the path. He did not touch the body. He knew enough to know there was no need.

At 3.15 a.m. a light came on in Mr Pendry's bathroom opposite. A call of nature, Henry surmised. A pity it had not called earlier. Even then, Henry knew that a witness would have been useful.

44

Walter Godelee was lying awake in the guest bedroom when the phone rang. His wife, who had shared his bed for thirty-eight years, was asleep in the master bedroom on the floor below. His absence from the marital bed had been prompted not by a rift, but by Walter's cough, an insistent tickle that had disrupted their sleep for almost a week.

"Better that one of us gets some sleep," he had murmured an hour earlier, picking up his watch and reading glasses from the bedside table.

His wife had raised her head from the pillow wondering why it had taken him five nights to do the decent thing.

"Oh darling," she said, "do you have to? Don't go on my account."

As the door clicked she sighed and pulled up the covers. She was asleep before he had reached the top landing.

He had lifted the phone on the first ring knowing that pre-dawn calls to solicitors always mean trouble.

Henry had said he was speaking from Chelsea police station and gave Walter a description of his history with Bateman and of the night's events.

"Have you been arrested?"

"Yes, I've been cautioned and told there will be a formal interview. They said I could ring a solicitor. I am so sorry to disturb your sleep."

"No, I'm sorry you've had such a hellish time."

He reached for his watch and made a quick calculation.

"I'll be with you in twenty minutes. Try not to worry. I know the arrest is alarming, but it's not unusual in this situation. When I get there, we're allowed a private session before we go into the interview room – so sit tight and say nothing.'

In truth, Walter was not as relaxed as he sounded. Why the hell had Henry not called him earlier, immediately after ringing 999? He must have known he would be questioned at the scene. The trouble with law-abiding citizens, he thought, as he bent to pull on his socks, is that they have no fear. They charge into the hidden cannons of the law in the mistaken belief that innocence makes them inviolate.

Despite what he had said to reassure Henry, the arrest was not merely a matter of form. There must have been something in Henry's initial responses to make the police suspect him of unlawful killing. Walter knew his client. In these circumstances better to have a client full of callow fear than righteous indignation. He had represented Henry throughout his divorce proceedings and knew he was capable of self-defeating anger.

Walter was shown straight into the interview room at the station. Henry seemed calm. He had been allowed to change out of his nightclothes (which had been labelled, bagged and taken away) and was wearing a suit, without a tie. A uniformed officer brought Walter a cup of coffee.

"You'll be needing this," he said with a straight face, closing the door quietly behind him.

Walter had taken out a legal pad and pen.

"Let me tell you what the situation is. The police can hold you here for twenty-four hours – then they must either charge you or release you. If they want to make further enquiries, or to consult the Crown Prosecution Service, they can release you on police bail on condition that you return at a set date."

Henry nodded, but did not ask a question. Walter continued, deliberately impersonal and matter of fact. He wanted Henry to be aware that he was now in the land of due process – that every utterance had a consequence – that no question would be casual and no answer should be unguarded.

"In my opinion, in the light of your previous encounters with Bateman, release on bail pending further enquiries is possible, but we'll see."

Henry looked up. "It was self-defence."

"Yes, I have no doubt that it was." Walter's tone was warmer. They were entering the crucial stage of their session.

"However, it isn't straightforward and before we go in for the interview, I want you to understand what in law justifies a plea of self-defence. I mean, really understand, for there is only one justification and if you stray from it, we have no case."

Walter paused to let the words sink in.

"Your only defence is that you perceived a threat to yourself and then took reasonable steps to defend yourself."

"Well, I was threatened. He had the saw in his hand."

"Yes . . . but there will be a question of whether he intended to use it."

"What was I meant to do – wait until my throat had been cut, just to be certain?"

Walter was patient. "This is where the concept of reasonable behaviour applies – the law would agree that it would be unreasonable for your swing of the bat to be posthumous."

"I took the same view."

"Nevertheless, I want you to be prepared for the kind of questions you'll get. Some of them will sound hostile, but they will not be inappropriate. The police will be interested in your state of mind when you swung the bat. If they believe you acted in anger, or with a sense of revenge, they will probably charge you."

"What should I say?"

"Tell them the truth. I'm not coaching you – I'm just pointing out that it's no defence in law to be angry or vengeful, but it is a defence to feel threatened and fearful."

Henry looked troubled. "What if there are mixed feelings?"

"There often are, but there's always a predominant one. Would you have hit him if he had dropped the saw?"

"No."

"The rose would still have been destroyed? There would still have been the months of persecution? You would have still been angry?"

"Yes, but . . ."

"But you wouldn't have felt under threat."

"I see."

"They will also be interested in whether your degree of self-protection was reasonable. A baseball bat is classed as an offensive weapon and they will make a judgment on whether its use was excessive."

"Jesus, I'm the victim here. He attacked me."

"A man is dead, Henry. There have to be questions."

"Yes, I can see that."

"It would also be helpful to have on record your regret at the outcome of the evening, that is, if you feel it. Which I am sure you do."

"I wanted him gone, not dead. I hit him on the shoulder. I didn't aim for his head."

For the first time, Henry looked upset. The adrenalin rush had subsided and he hung his head to hide his tears. He had killed a man, not intentionally, but it had happened.

Walter talked on, repeating some of his earlier points, giving Henry time to recover.

Two detectives conducted the interview. Cautions were issued and the session was recorded. Henry had seen the scene so often on television that he found it hard to take the proceedings seriously.

The leading questioner was Detective Inspector Harkness, a young man with a Birmingham accent and gelled hair, just too long to be spiky. Henry assumed that he had entered the force as a graduate and spent very little time in a helmet. He was wearing a black suit and was buttoned up in more ways than one.

"Mr Cage, could you tell us again what actual damage the victim had done to your property before you challenged him earlier this morning?"

"He had destroyed a rose at the front of my house."

"A rose bush?"

"Strictly speaking, it's a climber, not a bush."

"But it is just a plant, is it not? Not particularly uncommon or valuable?"

"No."

"Do you consider that arming yourself with a baseball bat and wielding it with fatal consequences was a reasonable response to the loss of a rose?" He paused. "Be it bush or climber . . . ?"

"I didn't strike him because of the rose. I hit him because he was about to attack me with the saw."

"Quite. How high had Bateman lifted the saw when you hit him?"

"I don't know. I saw the movement and reacted. As I said, I thought he was going to strike me."

Unexpectedly, Harkness stood up, pushing back his chair.

"How would he have done that with a nine-inch blade? Lifted it high and brought it down on you, like a sabre?"

He mimed the action.

"I don't think so, do you? Not much momentum – not with a nine-inch blade – and he would have to have been very, very close to you to cause any damage. More likely, if he had intended you harm, he would have thrust the saw at you as with a dagger – like so."

He pushed his arm forward in a series of fast, jabbing movements before sitting down.

He was out of breath and waited a few moments before continuing.

"You might have been in danger from a forward movement of his arm but there was no forward movement, was there? You say he only *raised* his arm, is that correct?"

"I saw his arm move upwards. I didn't know whether it was a prelude to a thrust or a slash. I was alarmed and swung the bat."

Walter was pleased. Henry was staying on strategy.

Harkness picked up a file and began turning the pages. The silence was stagy, an obvious attempt to ratchet up the tension.

"I see you have quite a history with Bateman, Mr Cage. Undoubtedly, an unpleasant man who has been persecuting you for many months. From the records it seems, sadly, we have not been able to give you the protection you deserved. You must have felt frustrated about that?"

"At times, yes. But I accept that the police need proof before they can act."

"It must have made you angry?"

"I was angry with Bateman, not the police."

"And were you still angry in the garden this morning? You said in your earlier statement that you were angry that he had killed a rose that you and your ex-wife" – he looked down at the paper to get the name right – "Nessa had planted thirty years ago. I understand that she has recently passed away. I'm sorry to hear that."

He closed the file.

"So how did you feel when you saw what he had done to something that obviously meant a lot to you – had meant a lot to both of you?"

The ploy was obvious; a cheap attempt to unsettle him, to play on his emotions and Henry knew the appropriate response.

"Upset" was the word he should use; a passive, reasonable, woolly-cardigan kind of a word, but it did not describe what Henry had felt. Even anger did not do justice to his feelings; he had felt rage – a searing, vindictive rage. The destruction of the rose had seemed like an attack on Nessa, on their history together.

"I was very angry."

"Were you still angry when you struck him?"

"I thought he was going to attack me with the saw."

"Were you still angry when you swung the bat into his head?"

"I didn't swing the bat at his head. I hit his shoulder, the bat bounced up and hit his head."

"You have not answered my question, Mr Cage. Were you still angry when you hit him?"

Henry hesitated. He was one word away from safety, but to say it would have been an oversimplification. He had to be accurate.

"I wasn't particularly self-aware at the time. It was not a moment for introspection."

Henry had not quite kept the sneer out of his voice.

"I repeat the question, Mr Cage. Were you angry when you hit him? All I need is a yes or no."

"It's not that black and white. Of course, I was angry, but I wouldn't have swung the bat if he had not raised the saw. I thought he was going to attack me. I knew he was a violent man."

45

After the breakfast rush and before the lunch crowd arrived, Jack usually had a cup of coffee at one of the outside tables. It was the time of day when Nessa used to drop by and every day he missed her company. Not that he was ever alone for long. His regulars, seeing the empty chairs at the table and ignoring the newspaper spread out before him, would often sit down and join him.

"Jack, thank God you're still here – everyone at the hotel is new. Nobody knows me!"

He looked up, the croaky voice familiar.

"I hear you're still smoking, Joan. How you doing?"

He pulled out a chair for her. Every summer, Joan and her husband came to the Ritz Carlton for three weeks, and every day they crossed the boulevard for a late breakfast at Jack's.

"Where's Warren – getting the newspapers?"

"I guess he's in New York." She hesitated. "We've split up."

He looked at her for signs of damage, but everything seemed as normal. She wore her silver hair cropped close to the skull and it suited her. She was a pixie of a woman, in her early sixties and still trim. He assumed she had been the one to pull the plug.

"I'm sorry to hear that. You guys were together for a long time."

"Thirty-four years." She shook her head in wonder. "We separated last month. We flew back from California and I asked him to move out. But life goes on, and here I am, business as usual."

Arlene brought over coffee and a smoked salmon bagel for Joan.

"Good to have you back."

They air-kissed and Arlene, sensing some seriousness in the air, moved off.

"So what happened?" Jack was curious.

"We had a row." She paused. "About Scrabble."

"Scrabble?"

"I know, I know – everyone laughs. But listen to this and tell me if I'm wrong. The man's not all there, believe me."

She took a bite out of her bagel and Jack had to wait. She would not talk with her mouth full.

"Before Warren would play a game, he had to empty the bag and count all the Scrabble letters – every last one of them. For years he's been doing it. I said to him in the hotel; why do you do that? It's driving me nuts. You put them back in the bag yourself just three hours ago – you think there's a Scrabble thief in the Bel Air?"

She took a gulp of coffee.

"So he says, 'When I play, I like to play with a full set of letters. I like to be sure, that's all. What is it? A crime?' So I let him have it. Yes, you shit, it is. It's the crime of obsession. It's the crime of being a jerk. I'm as mad as all hell, and he just goes on counting and explaining. 'Let's say I'm holding a Q and I know there are four U tiles and three of them are already in play, then I know there's a fourth U in the bag, so I hang on to the Q in the hope of getting the remaining U, but if the fucking U is on the carpet, then I make the wrong fucking decision, see?'"

Jack is laughing and she smiles.

"Don't tell me."

"So, it's over?"

"He's coming down at the weekend. He wants to talk."

"Bring him over for breakfast. I don't like to think of you two apart."

She put her hand on his arm.

"Anyhow, that's enough about me. How have you been? How's my friend Nessa?"

He was just about to tell her when his cell phone rang. He excused himself, glad to put off the moment.

He took the call on the move, walking away from the tables and into the car park. When he came back to the table, he looked stunned.

"A friend of mine in London has been arrested for murder. Some guy came at him with a knife and he was just defending himself. Jesus, it doesn't make sense."

"That's dreadful," Joan said, thinking not of Jack's friend, but of Warren, alone in New York and, perhaps, in peril.

46

Henry's arrest did not entirely surprise Walter, but he remained confident that the charge would be dropped when the Crown Prosecution Service had gathered more evidence. He had hoped that Henry would have been granted bail pending further investigations, but it was not unreasonable for the C.P.S. to treat the evidence at this stage as prima facie. He could understand their reasoning.

Henry had killed a trespasser, not a burglar. Colin Bateman had made no attempt to enter Henry's house, and it was reasonable to assume that he would have left the garden after destroying the rose had he not been discovered. It was self-evident that he had brought the saw to cut through the trunk of the rose and not as an offensive weapon. The enterprise had been carried out at night. He had not expected to meet Mr Cage, let alone attack him. There had been no intent to harm. In contrast, Mr Cage had armed himself with a baseball bat before leaving the house, and presumably had been prepared to use it. By his own admission, he had been angry when striking Bateman. Since there had been no witness to the events in question, there was only Henry's word that Bateman had threatened to use the saw as a weapon. On the face of it, a man had been bludgeoned to death for tampering with a rose bush. Walter conceded that there was a case to answer.

The police had pressed for the arrest on a charge of murder and the Crown Prosecution Service had agreed. At 2.00 p.m., Henry had appeared before a magistrate and had been remanded in custody at Brixton Prison.

(His appearance in court did not go unnoticed by the media.)

For the next thirty days, Henry was an absentee from his own life. He was not at St Mary's Cadogan for the christening of Ivy Elizabeth, his friend Oliver's granddaughter. He was not at the Albert Hall to hear Jessye Norman sing – and when England dismissed the West Indies for sixty-one runs in their second innings at Headingley, Henry was not on his feet in the pavilion, but sitting in his cell, two hundred miles away.

And then, more or less on the day that Walter had predicted, the C.P.S. had advised that no charges were to be brought against Mr Henry Cage. He was to be released immediately, with no stain on his character.

The decision was greeted with qualified approval. The *Guardian* was in no doubt that the finding was sound, but felt that in reaching this verdict the C.P.S. had laid itself open to the suspicion that they had one law for the rich and another for the poor. *The Times*, acknowledging that the defence of self-defence was finely nuanced, had argued for more consistency in the rulings and an urgent review of the code that guided its decisions.

The *Daily Mirror*'s reaction was less measured – CAGE FREE AS FARMER ROTS IN JAIL!

The farmer in question was named Tony Martin. A few months earlier, in a controversial trial, he had been found guilty of murder despite a similar plea of self-defence. Mr Martin had been disturbed at his remote farmhouse by two intruders. He had fired his shotgun into the darkness and had hit the young men. One of them had died from two shots in the back and the other had been hit in the leg. Mr Martin, an elderly man living alone, had claimed that he had felt under threat and had blasted away, hoping to scare off the trespassers. The jury, invited to weigh the evidence that the young men had been running *away* from the house when shot, had found Mr Martin guilty of murder. The verdict had been widely criticised and was now under appeal. Most of the media and many lawyers anticipated that the sentence would be reduced to one of manslaughter.

Henry had asked if the Martin case would influence his own case. Walter believed it would not, in itself, make any difference.

"They will only bring charges if they believe there is enough evidence to result in a guilty verdict – it is as simple as that. But it's true that the Martin trial has made self-defence high-profile and I'm sure your case will be pulled apart by everyone right up to the D.P.P. himself."

In that Walter was proved right. When the papers reached the Director of Public Prosecutions an informal commentary from a senior prosecutor was attached to the summary page of the official recommendation:

In my opinion, no jury will consign Henry Cage to prison based on this evidence. Any prosecution would be unsafe; I believe we must let Mr Cage get on with his life.

The forensic report confirms that the bat had struck the victim's shoulder before bouncing on to the temple. This is consistent with Mr Cage's insistence that he had been trying to thwart the attack and not kill the attacker.

You will see that Detective Sergeant Cummings' report confirms that Bateman had a history of violent behaviour going back over ten years. He has recently interviewed Eileen Fisher, Bateman's ex-girlfriend, and she testifies that he still had an explosive temper and frequently struck her. She witnessed Bateman's assault of Cage on Westminster Bridge on New Year's Eve and even more damning, she claims that Bateman had admitted hammering a masonry pin through the skull of a dog to even a score. (I suggest, unlikely to endear him to a British jury.)

Cummings reveals, as you will see in the footnote, that the dog's owner had sought to bring charges against Bateman, but at that time, Miss Fisher had not had the conversation with Bateman and had provided an alibi.

Mrs Connie Bateman, the victim's mother, and Miss Julia Hughes, the victim's aunt, have also provided statements citing Bateman's violence at home.

Mr Dave Clarke from Apex Scaffolding, claims that Bateman had attacked him with a short pole on a building site in February 2000. There were several witnesses to the assault, but Mr Clarke had decided not to press charges.

It is understood all three women and Mr Clarke have agreed to be witnesses for the defence, if Mr Cage is charged.

Perhaps even more significantly, D.S. Cummings supplies the minutes of a meeting with Mr Cage on 20 June, 2000, at which Mr Cage identified Bateman as the man who had attacked him on Westminster Bridge on New Year's Eve.

D.S. Cummings informed Mr Cage of Bateman's record. The defence would certainly use this to suggest that Mr Cage had good reason to believe on the fateful night that an armed Bateman was capable of the most serious violence.

At the same meeting, Cummings reports that Mr Cage had announced his intention of leaving London to live near his family in Norfolk. He was selling his London house and was anxious to put himself out of harm's way and lead a more peaceful life. Not the posture of a vengeful man, I can hear the defence saying.

There is a lot more for you to weigh, but I am satisfied, having read it all, that Mr Cage genuinely felt that he was under threat and took reasonable steps to defend himself.

I'm sorry I couldn't get this to you earlier in the day. You weren't planning to go out this evening, were you?

47

Jack had stocked up the fridge and prepared the bed in Nessa's room. He was not adroit at hospital folds and looking back from the door, the bed had reminded him of the books he wrapped at Christmas, taut over the flat surfaces but a rumpled mess at either end. Still, he did not imagine Henry would object after his recent sleeping quarters.

It had been Tom's idea that Henry should fly to Florida on the day of his release.

"Stay for a few weeks," he had said, "until things calm down here. Jack will open up the house in Florida and Jane and I will handle the move to Norfolk."

Not wanting to be recognised, Henry had shaved his head on his last day in Brixton. In fact, his looks had already changed, altered by one of those ageing spurts brought on by a fall or an operation – or a month in prison. At arrivals, he had seen Jack and walked straight past him. As the last stragglers left the baggage hall and Jack was getting anxious, Henry had tugged on his sleeve from behind.

"Jesus, no wonder I didn't spot you. Why the convict look – I thought you had got off?"

Henry had been annoyed, unprepared for Jack's

breeziness, but had said nothing. In the car, he had closed his eyes, pretending to be asleep.

At the house, Jack handed over the keys.

"There's stuff in the fridge and you know where I am. Come over when you're ready."

Henry had ignored Jack for two weeks. When the food in the fridge ran out, he ordered pizza.

Tom called every other day at noon and Henry talked to Hal. In the afternoons he walked on the beach. In the evenings he slept in front of the television.

Jack waited it out. When Henry finally came over for breakfast, Jack was ready with an apology.

"I'm sorry. I have a fast tongue and a feeble brain. It's a bad combination, I know."

He reached out to shake Henry's hand.

As the weeks passed, Henry relaxed a little and Jack asked him about his time in prison.

"I wouldn't recommend it, but at least it was a hiding place. No cameras or reporters."

At first he had been fearful. He had anticipated hostility from the other inmates. A bookish, middle-class man, known to be well off, he had imagined himself an obvious target. But he had been wrong. He had been ignored. Overcrowding meant that the prisoners were confined to their cells for most of the day and time dragged. Boredom worked like bromide in the tea; nobody gave a toss who you were or what you had done.

The only relief came with visitors. Walter was there most days and Tom or Jane once a week. Charles England had visited twice, bearing books and magazines. On his first visit he had brought something else to show Henry.

"You won't like this, but don't worry. I've put a stop to it."

He had held up a white T-shirt with the bright-red legend: DON'T CAGE THE CAGE!

Charles had been amused by Henry's pained expression.

"The plan was for all the staff to march on Downing Street. Can you imagine? Not Henry's style, I told them, but the sentiment would be appreciated."

One afternoon, Walter had arrived in a sober suit and a black tie.

"I went to Bateman's cremation this morning. I thought you would want me to."

"Thank you."

It had been a brief, dry-eyed affair. Colin's mother, his aunt and Walter had been the only mourners. Outside, on the square metre of paving reserved for Bateman's floral tributes, his mother had left a defiant bouquet, a gaudy mix of dissonant blooms and hues. Mrs Bateman had been insistent that the florist should pack in as many colours as possible.

Three days before Henry's release, Maude had come to see him. She had talked about Nessa. She had read all the obituaries and had loved seeing the old photographs. "She was very beautiful."

As she left, she told him she was thinking of moving on again, perhaps to live and work in Paris for a while. She thought she might find work in a gallery. After all, she did have a degree in art history. She had not promised to send him her new address, nor had she mentioned how easy it would be to take the Eurostar and join her for lunch in Paris – but in the lingering scent of her perfume, Henry had pictured himself making the trip.

Only once during his stay in Florida did Henry discuss the death of Bateman. They were in the car driving to Palm Beach for a Saturday night concert.

"I sometimes think it was meant to happen. There were thousands of people on Westminster Bridge that night and I was shoved into Bateman. Why him?"

"I don't know."

"Perhaps he was my punishment?"

"For what?"

Henry's answer had been almost inaudible.

"My various failings."

"It was wrong time, wrong place – that's all, Henry. There's no big finger pointing down from the sky."

Jack had slowed on a tight bend. Around the corner was the entrance to Donald Trump's mansion and there were often limousines lined up, waiting to turn into the driveway. Once past the house, Jack had eased the car back to 30 miles per hour.

"Shit happens, Henry, it just happens. You think Nessa *deserved* her cancer?"

"No, Jack, I don't."

Henry had reached across and turned on the radio – the snap of the control as sharp as his reply. As fate would have it, Tom Waits was singing "Looking for the Heart of Saturday Night".

The conversation was never resumed.

In England the news circus had moved on, but still

Henry delayed his return. Tom and Jane had invited him to become a partner in the bookshop. They were hoping to have another child and were already looking for a house. The flat over the shop was too small and the business could take over the space and expand. They needed help and would he think about it, please?

He had been non-committal, knowing that his hesitation was hurtful. Why had he bought the Norfolk house if he did not want to be part of their lives?

Even when Hal begged him to return, he was evasive.

"Soon Hal, it won't be long."

It was caution that kept him in Florida. His hair had grown back and he had put on weight; he looked more like his old self, but he had lost his nerve. In Palm Beach he was anonymous; in Norfolk, he feared he would be notorious.

The weather had turned humid, and each night before going to bed, Henry walked from the house into the ocean, stopping only when the water reached his chest. It was here, at this depth, that they had scattered Nessa's ashes, just as she had wished. And it was here, one night, with perhaps some vestige of her still by his side, that Henry Cage had closed his eyes and prayed for guidance.

Unexpectedly, it came the next day from Mrs Abraham.

Dear Mr Cage,

I hope you don't mind me writing. I wanted to thank you properly for the money and I'm not sure I ever did, and it's been on my mind. Tom said it would be alright to write. During the move, he showed me a photo of Hal. There's a lot of Mr Cage in him, I said, and there is – well, I think so. I expect you can't wait to get back and see him. Best regards, Peggy. (Mrs Abraham)

What was it she had said to him that day in the kitchen?

"But what about you, Mr Cage? Didn't *you* want to be with her for every single minute she had left?"

That had been the gist of it and she had been right to chide him. He had not been with Nessa for her last minutes. He had not even been there for her last hours, days, or weeks. He had been on the wrong side of the Atlantic – just like now.

When he rang, it was Jane who answered the phone.

"If the offer is still on, I would love to be part of the bookshop . . . and everything else."

"Oh Henry, wait there, don't go away . . ."

He heard her calling upstairs. He looked at his watch, it must be Hal's bath time – her voice was triumphant.

"Hal, Tom, he's coming, he's coming!"

She was back on the line. "He's just wrapping a towel around Hal – you wouldn't believe the joy."

When Tom took over the phone, Henry could hear an excited Hal in the background. He was laughing and clapping his hands – welcoming Henry (at long last) on to the dance floor.

Acknowledgements

My thanks to Alan Stoker for helping me understand the nature and treatment of cancer. Jerome Goodman's compassionate article in the *New Yorker* (25 October, 2002) was instructive about the last days of a terminal illness. John Fraser guided me through the legal niceties of "self-defence" and much more. On a lighter note, Peter Pettinger's wonderful book *How My Heart Sings* taught me much about Bill Evans, as did Peter Keepnews' record notes for *Milestones*. Mike Dempsey inspired the jacket design and Frank Lieberman tracked down the Orson Welles tape. I thank them both. John de Falbe and Justin Cartwright were the first to see the completed manuscript of this book and their encouragement (and advice) was uplifting at a critical time. Later, I could not have been more fortunate in having Christopher MacLehose as both my publisher and editor. As an editor Christopher belongs in the same sentence as Max Perkins and William Maxwell. Alongside him at MacLehose Press, Katharina Bielenberg has tolerated my indecision and been a charming and erudite guide. I thank, too, Sarah Barlow, proofreader, Patty Rennie, typesetter, and Nick Johnston at Quercus for his unfailing help. Finally, my thanks and love to Eve and my family.